Eight Doors

Foster

Eight Doors supports ManHealth, a not-for-profit CIC who run free peer-support groups and a live WebChat seven nights a week from 6-10pm via their website for men struggling with mental health conditions. They also provide training around health inequalities for men and mental health. Their peer support groups and WebChat are all run by male facilitators who have a lived experience. They know that talking to people who have been through similar challenges may: help you to talk about what you are feeling and experiencing; help you share suggestions for coping techniques and support options; Introduce you to ideas and approaches that have been helpful to others; reassure you that you're not the only person who has felt like this.

info@manhealth.org.uk

www.manhealth.org.uk

Profound loss doesn't end, unfortunately. It continues; it creeps into your thoughts and conversations forever.

Yet this book is meant to be daft. Being silly *in* awful situations is what gets us through them, and I think being silly here may just be what reminds someone of a better time, of better people and that they are important to so many more people than they probably realise. This is all about the characters' interactions, so don't expect flamboyant descriptions; do expect profanity and idiocy. Being silly may *prevent* awful situations.

The story here (again) is exactly that: a story. However, almost every character is named after somebody real, and modelled loosely on someone who existed - which absolutely does not mean they did the things written here. Please, if you know Kev, stop asking about his bowels! The setting, too, is based very much on a real place. The reason for these choices is that this is a real 'story', very close to my heart, and very much part of my world. If you read Nine Doors, it probably feels like part of yours now too.

On that note, Nine Doors really does precede events here. You don't have to read it, but a lot of the actions are consequences from events in the first book - a lot of the jokes are continuations of previous conversations. Eight Doors follows directly, and as such the characters are already fully formed.

In loving, twisted memory of
Jamie Buck **(2018)** & Lee Hoar **(2019)**

And with immense love for
Ruche van der Mescht
(2012)

Thank you to my amazing wife, Cass, for encouraging me, and to all of the beautiful people who wanted to know more about these characters for your ongoing support.

Kev Palmer, Ste Mitchell, Darren Hughes, Marc Holehouse, Stuart Cook, Stuart Hedley - thank you for becoming awful characters that people seem to like – more than your real versions.

To my daughters, we *can* make a difference, even in the most unusual of ways. Read this at 18.

Nine Doors & Eight Doors are both available from
www.do9rs.co.uk
where £5 from every paperback is donated to charity.

Please review on Amazon, follow the pages below, and share as much as you can.
Facebook = @NineDo9rs
Twitter = @NineDo9rs
Instagram = ninedoorsnovel

Prologue 7
Chapter 1: Doors 8
Chapter 2: Pick-up 17
Chapter 3: Crem 21
Chapter 4: Wake 26
Chapter 5: Taxi 33
Chapter 6: Group Chat 38
Chapter 7: Outing 40
Chapter 8: Taking the Michael 48
Chapter 9: Bet 60
Interlude: 67
Chapter 10: Friday, 18:00 69
Chapter 11: Friday, 19:00 75
Chapter 12: Friday, 19:30 78
Chapter 13: Friday: 19:45 81
Chapter 14: Friday, 20:00 84
Chapter 15: Friday, 20:15 86
Chapter 16: Friday, 20:30 91
Chapter 17: Friday, 20:45 93
Chapter 18: Friday, 21:00 98
Chapter 19: Friday, 21:15 100
Chapter 20: Friday, 21:20 103
Chapter 21: Friday, 21:30 106
Chapter 22: Friday, 22:00 108
Chapter 23: Saturday, 20:00 112
Chapter 24: Saturday, 20:15 116
Chapter 25: Saturday, 20:45 121
Chapter 26: 1995 123
Chapter 27: Saturday, 21:00 135

Chapter 28: Saturday, 21:00 137
Chapter 29: Saturday, 21:10 139
Chapter 30: Saturday, 21:20 142
Chapter 31: 1974 143
Chapter 32: Canter 145
Chapter 33: Coffees 149
Chapter 34: Cem 158
Gaz: 1995 160

Prologue

Shattering across the floor, the photograph of them fishing together - which seemed eternities ago now - flew from the wall as the door struggled to hold back the force slamming against it.

'I'm sorry, I'm sorry! Please…'

'Open this fucking door you little shit…mark me words…'

'No, I'm sorry! Calm down, please…'

'Calm down? Calm fu...right!'

Silence spilled into the room. Crushed against the farthest wall, between the foot of the bed and the wardrobe, a second to breathe settled.

'Oh, than…'

The door fell forwards, crashing onto the rug and rattling the toys and keepsakes on the shelves. Propelled by momentum and rage, the beast lay on top of it in the centre of the room. Then, it was onto all fours, then knees, then stood.

Then *moving*.

Chapter 1: Doors

The bar was almost empty, except for one old man whose hearing aid was out of batteries and emitting a high-pitched screech, and the barman. It was one of those pubs that think they're cooler than they are, with life-affirming slogans in gold calligraphy on the overhead beams. Queen's 'Now I'm Here' played quietly, just audible amongst the clinking of glasses in the washer and the hearing aid.

The bar was boat-shaped in the centre of the room, with booths on both sides. At a booth on the side closest to the entrance, in jeans and a 'Heaven is a Halfpipe' t-shirt, stroking his beard, sat Kev. They'd arranged to meet at one o'clock but he'd been waiting since twenty to, with one eye on the glass double doors.

The barman, a spotty, gangly creature with the attitude of a maitre de at a swanky restaurant but the odour of a chronic masturbator, was laughing to himself as he scrolled through his phone.

'That noise not bother you?' asked Kev.

'What? Oh, Rocketman? No, used to it, in here *every* day!'

'Rocketman?'

'Yeah, it sounds like the bit where he's singing 'hiiiiii-ighhhhhh as a kite', you know?'

'Fair enough, does it not get busy in…'

Kev was cut off by a crash from the direction of the doorway, and turned to see Mitch angrily yanking at the handle, before trying the other door and walking in muttering to himself.

'You need a sign on that door, kid!'

'There is one!'

'There fucking *isn't*!'

'There *is* - it says 'Please use other door'.

By this point Mitch had gone back to the door, opened it, looked at the sign saying 'Please use other door' and turned back toward the bar.

'Carling.'

'Please?'

'Don't push it!

'Mitch, you alright?'

'Bloody hell, what're you doing here already, I thought I'd be the first!'

'Just keen to get here and see you lot again!'

'It's only been a week!'

'Yeah, but it felt right being back together, you know?'

'Aye, it did...speaking of, I'm seeing Marie again.'

'Nice one.'

Mitch picked up his pint, paid and then said 'here's Lee!' just before he walked straight into the door.

'Did you do that as well, Kev?'

'Oh, yes.'

'Lads, how's it going! *You*, you need to put a sign on that door!'

'There is one!' replied the barman.

'Bollocks is there, where is it then...oh...okay. Sorry, pal. Can I have a coke please?'

'It's Pepsi!'

'Right, can I have one then?'

'He's dressed better this time', Kev whispered to Mitch.

'No shit!'

'Exactly!'

'You two alright then?'

'Yeah mate, good. You?'

Alright, yeah - still not properly got my head around it that...'

'Here you go!'

'What you giving him *that* for?'

'He bet me we'd hear your catchphrase before you'd *even* sat down!'

'Thank you!' said Kev, taking Mitch's money with delight.

'I'm serious you know, it's really playing on my mind all the time!'

'Same, mate - we're just messing.'

Everyone, including the barman, looked to the door as Hughesy's face collided with it. There followed a moment where it seemed he was working out why the door had attacked him, and then he opened the other one.

'How's your bad head, mate?'

'Funny, aye - I was looking at me phone - they need a sign on that door!'

'There is one', muttered the barman without looking up.

The others nodded, and Hughesy looked back at the door.

'Who were you texting? Were you onto Fragille Rock to see if they wanted to take your kids back?'

'Very good...I was trying Gaz again, I've messaged him three times reminding him about today.'

'His phone still knackered, then!'

'Speaking of, it's no surprise Jabba the Pizza Hut isn't here yet.'

'He'll be ages, Greggs doesn't close until after five!'

'Haha, he's not the only one missing though, give him a chance!'

A familiar thud echoed across the room, momentarily overpowering the constant screech of the hearing aid and muffled sounds of Queen's 'Seven Seas of Rhye'.

'You need a sign on that door, young'un!'

'There is one. Can none of you rea…'

The barman stopped speaking as he looked up to see Bucky before him, cap pulled down just above his eyes with one human arm and one massively swollen, deep purple one.

'...what happened to your arm?'

'I walked into your stupid door! Pint of lager.'

'Which one?'

'What you got?'

'Stella Armtois, Armstel, Pero-no, San Migfuckinghell…'

'You can piss off, pulling at me and making it *worse*!'

'Woah', said Kev, feigning shock, 'you can't blame *me* for this!'

'What lager do you want?'

'Any! Sorry Kev, I know. It's just been over a week now and look at the state of this. I can't even wear a jacket to cover it up!'

'Why not?'

'Can't get my forearm through.'

'Well, if you need cheering up, watch Dave!'

They looked towards the door as Dave mounted the steps and then predictably jarred his arm pushing open a door that wouldn't move. He then tried the other door and walked straight over to the table.

'They need a sign on that door!' he said, rubbing his shoulder.

'There is one!' replied the barman, Kev, Mitch, Hughesy, Lee, Bucky and the old man.

'Fair enough, how are you faggots?'

'Thought we talked about the homophobic comments?' whispered Mitch.

'I'm not homophobic, man!'

'You're so homophobic you might be protesting too much, Dave', added Lee.

'Dave, pint?' shouted Bucky from the bar.

'Please mate - cider!'

'Ooh, can't believe you'd ever want cider again after last weekend!'

'Got a taste for it - real cider, though, not that blue-bottled turps we were drinking!'

'Gentlemen', boomed Cookie as he walked through the same door they had all tried.

'Cookie, lad!'

'You've broken the door!'

'Have I?'

'Yeah, it was locked and *you've* just snapped it.'

'Okay...sorry!'

'You will have to pay for it, I'll ring the manager!'

'Look kid, I said sorry! If you didn't want people to push it you should have put a sign on the thing!'

'There is one!'

'Is there? Oh yeah.'

'What sort of an idiot...'

'No mate, don't do it!'

'Quiet, little one!'

'He's a gonner!'

Cookie leant over the bar, so his face was close to the barman's. Until now, he had been looking at the broken door more than the giant approaching him. He gulped.

'I said sorry. I am *trying* to be a nice guy. I am *not* going to get angry. But you *need* to shut up, now.'

The barman skulked off into the other corner and pretended to wipe some tables.

Cookie reached across, filled a glass with water from the soft drinks gun, and joined the others around the table.

'Where's Knacker and Gaz?'

'We've been trying to reach Gaz, but no joy. Knacker is his usual self.'

'He said he was here ages ago!'

'Gaz?'

'No, Knacker. We've spoken a few times since last week. Text me about half twelve saying he was *already* here!'

'I've been here since not long after that!' said Kev.

'Has the berk gone to the wrong place again?'

'Well, he can blame Gaz again seeing as his phone's *still* fucked!'

'He saw the messenger conversation though - Gaz did. Everyone's viewed it, so he knows where we are and when, even if he can't answer his mobile or get texts.'

'He'll turn up then.'

'Wey aye.'

'What about Knacker though, send out a search party?'

'Wouldn't take much searching!'

'Haha he's that big we can shout Knacker and he'll be nearby at all times, man!'

'Knacker!!!'

'Yeah?' came the reply.

'What sort of magic is this?'

'He's here, the prick!'

'Coming 'round lads!'

'Did you not look around the other side of the bar when you got here, like, Kev?'

'I was that early I didn't think anyone else'd be here, did I?'

'To be fair, I'm surprised he wasn't sticking out both sides of the bar!'

'Hey, lads. Been waiting ages. You all been here long? You've got drinks!'

'Yeah, sorry, we didn't realise you were over *that* side.'
'Bit out of the way, Knacker, who you hiding from?'
'Barman.'
'Why?'
'I broke the bloody door and he rang the manager - it was too late to ring anyone and change venue - he was gonna put a sign on!'
'There is one!'
'Yeah, there's a sign!'
'He did!'
'I just tripped on the steps and fell into the thing...wouldn't stay shut so he had to lock it.'
'Lads', said Hughesy, 'I hate to be the one who starts the serious conversations…'
'It'll make a change from *always* being me!', said Bucky. 'Sick of being the mature intellectual one!'
'You can take a turn being the fat one', added Knacker, 'one arm is already trying!'
'Dick!'
'Go on, Hughesy, bud! Think we've all got serious thoughts we want to get out, as well as a good laugh.'
'I don't know if you'll all remember but when I was little my uncle died, and I've recently found out it was...you know, he took his own life. With Foz as well I've just spent a lot of time thinking about it.'
'You alright, mate?'
'Yeah, I'm good. It was thirty-odd years ago, it's just made me more aware of how prevalent it is, so I've done some courses.'
'Golf?'
'Ha I wish. I advocate talking about mental health, mental illness and suicide prevention at work, right! Everyone knows why it's *so* important to me! Anyway, this woman said her daughter was saying the world would be better off without her, and that she wanted to kill herself, and asked me to chat to her.'
'Woah, really?'
'Yeah - I said I've done some courses like CAMHS and MHFA, but I'm not a professional. She said no, please, you

will understand her. So I did it, one evening. We talked about everything - speaking to her doctor, to CALM or Samaritans, to her friends properly - I talked about getting active, getting out, changing her routine, we talked about when she feels this way and how she can see it coming and ring her Ma or something *before* it's too negative. I basically told her a dozen things she can do to avoid or deal with it, really pushing *asking* for professional help!'

'What happened?'

'She's fine - I don't know if she did any of that stuff, or if it was just something she was saying; I asked her straight out how she planned to end her own life…'

'Brutal!'

'…it's not! If someone wants to die we *can't* be scared of asking if they've got a plan of how they will do it. They probably have considered method if they're serious! Too many young people, and this is part of the issue about understanding mental illness, say 'I've got so much homework I may as well kill myself!' You *what*? It is not a flippant statement, not a throwaway comment, and someone might *really* be thinking of doing that, of succumbing, and see your nonchalance as a reason not to speak up. Good mental health is happiness, according to your radio hosts and cereal boxes, so if you're not happy then you must have poor mental health, which must be the same as mental illness? No. Being unhappy, or being not ecstatic, are not the same thing. Am I banging on?'

'No mate, we're listening!'

'You're right too, being sad at times is natural!'

'What happened with the girl?'

'Sorry, yeah - like I said I don't know because the woman has a go at me at work. Apparently I *claim* to care about suicide prevention but I wasn't supportive, I just kept suggesting ways for her to challenge those feelings.'

'What did she want?'

'I think that's another big problem: if you advocate talking about it, surely you mean 'I am going to listen to everything you have to say then tell you everything I possibly can for you to try and do to live better' but this woman just wanted me to agree and say I understood and, I dunno, be fucking sad *with* her!'

'That wouldn't help!'

'It would reinforce those emotions, surely?'

'Exactly! I told her she was mistaken if she expected me to just join the pity party, and that all the advice I gave was in the best interests of her girl but she needed to speak to her doctor and get the right advice. Only she knows exactly what she's feeling and thinking so she *has to be* the one to make the change.' Hughesy breathed a sigh, having got more animated as he'd talked.

'Yeah, we can only do so much if they won't engage with help.'

'I see this 'it's okay not to be okay' slogan, you know, and it winds me up!', said Mitch.

'Right, why?'

'Because I agree with it and disagree with it in equal parts! I completely agree that if you do not feel okay then that's not something abnormal or taboo, but it's not okay to just feel like that and not know you can talk about it or act on it! I see that on t-shirts and hashtags and I want to tell whoever says it or wears it to add 'but if you're not, tell someone' underneath it!'

'I can't imagine feeling like everything is pointless and then seeing that it's acceptable written across some bird's tits!'

'Sexist!', added Knacker.

'It's okay to not feel okay as long as you're okay and are aware that it can be okay, okay!', suggested Lee.

'Perfect, but unless you're Knacker or LoLo Ferrari that's not fitting on a chest.'

'Anyway, apart from Gaz we're all here…'

'What a letdown!'

'His old man's probably grounded him again!'

'…so what's the plan?'

'Well, I was talking to Mitch and *we* thought…'

'Na, no way!'

'Not again!'

'Fuck off, Bucky!'

Chapter 2: Pick-up

'He won't pick up, never mind text back.'
'What, is his phone *on*?'
'Yeah, he answered last week, I think it was the Sunday after, you know, but he hung up!'
'Wanker.'
'He missed half the night didn't he - maybe he's just not bothered about knocking about together again.'
'No, when me, him and Hughesy left you lot he was talking about how good it had been, that he couldn't wait for the next one!'
'Yeah, he even said to me and Cookie that he felt more relaxed and at peace than he had for a long time, knowing he had his mates back. Even said he felt he was going to get a good night's kip for once.'
'Well, we'll see if he shows.'
'Barman's finally back, anyone for another?'
'Please, yeah.'
'Lager for me!'
'I'm good thanks!'
'What about you, Thanos arm?'
'Go on, then.'
'Lee, can I just say how lovely it is to have you within ten feet of us today!'
'Thanks. Let's just hope Cotton-Eye Hobo doesn't throw his faeces all over me!'
'There was no throwing involved!'
'Knacker, have you put this music on?'
'Yeah, there's a jukebox over the other side!'
'Have you only put Queen songs on?'
'No, no...I put 'Living On My Own' on as well!'
'By Freddie Mercury?'
'Yeah!'
'What an eclectic taste you have!'
'I know.'
I bet you'd even have Queen as your funeral song!'
'Morbid, but yeah!'
'Which?'

'Who Wants To Live Forever!'

'Foz's was Live Forever!'

'Oh yeah. What would yours be then?'

'I don't want to think about all your funeral songs, lads. I never want to go to another funeral in my life!'

'I agree, but can I just tell you all to listen to *Song For Josh* by Frank Turner - it's completely encapsulated how I feel!'

'I know that one - always been good but makes me break down *now* I've got the same experience. *One More Light* by Linkin Park is my go-to at the minute.'

'Okay, so we've compiled the world's most depressing fucking playlist...'

'So what's everyone's thoughts on last weekend?'

'The less the better?'

'I know it went awry a wee bit at times, but it was good wasn't it!'

'*Wee* bit?'

'We wouldn't have all come today...except Gaz the letdown...if it hadn't been good to get together again.'

'Tell you, boys, I have *needed* you lot in my life for God knows how long. Last weekend was awesome, even if I nearly got murdered to death by the Manson family.'

'Yeah it made me realise how strong these bonds are, that can never be broken.'

'Sames!'

'I would genuinely do anything for any one of you - and I think it's important that I say this out loud - I *love* you. You're the best friends I *ever* had!'

'That's...'

'Don't be homophobic, Dave!'

'I wasn't. I was gonna say that's my sentiments exactly, thank you very much. And while we are on that subject, there's something I really need to talk to you all about, even without Gaz here!'

'Ooh interesting!'

'You're emigrating?'

'Your wife's preggers?'

'No, lads...'

'You're gay!'

The rest of the lads roared with laughter, as a freshly waxed pickup truck pulled up beyond the broken glass door. The driver exited the vehicle and walked around to the back, out of sight, before reappearing with several crates of bottles on a dolly. He came in through the open door and started to speak to the barman, before his eyes drifted over the group to his left.

'Delivery mate...Rocketman's still here, eh...Lads, lads, *lads*!'

'Hey, Dicky!'

'What's up, Dicky mate?'

'Just full of busy - you lot not learnt your lesson from last weekend?'

'This is a quiet, mature get-together!'

'Good to hear; raising a glass, eh?'

'Yeah, I guess!'

'Dicky, I haven't been around with that cash yet...'

'I know! You can *definitely* fit it through the letterbox!'

'I've just been busy, you know!'

'So busy that you're in the pub?'

'I'll get it to you this week.'

Dicky left and returned with another stack of crates.

'Sorry for your loss, lads. He was a good, sound bloke. It's awful news.'

'We're still getting our heads around it.'

'I bet!'

'We had a nice send-off, paid our respects, you know!'

'Yeah - is the funeral tomorrow?'

'You what?'

'It was about four weeks ago now, Dicky son.'

'I'm confused! It was in the New Town News this week, the announcements...might have been today actually.'

'What was?'

'The funeral, up at the crem!'

'I hope his batshit Ma hasn't gone and arranged another service?'

'His Ma?' said Dicky. 'He was brought up by his Da wasn't he?'

'What the fuck is going on? Look, we were out last weekend to give Foz a proper send-off. The funeral was weeks ago but we missed it!'

'Except Gaz!'

'Aye, *except* Gaz!'

'What are you going on about?'

'There's a New Town on the bar there!'

Knacker picked up the newspaper and turned to the announcements section. His face froze. His chins kept moving for a second or two.

'Lads, I'm *so* sorry...I'm talking about *Gaz*!'

Chapter 3: Crem

Squeezed into the back of the pick-up, Kev, Hughesy, Bucky and Mitch re-read the announcement section to each other between Googling and trying to ring Gaz.

'His phone's on, man! Why's his fucking phone *on*?'

'You know what I said to him on the day of Foz's funeral? I said unless it was *his* own, he wouldn't be the only one of us who turned up'.

'You can't dwell on that, man.'

'Come on, that doesn't *mean* anything!'

'We'll get there on time!'

'It says here it started at two - it's five past now!'

'Wey, Dicky's driving like Miss Daisy but it's not far!'

'Surprised he's *not* speeding knowing we're in the back with all these bevvies!'

'I'll have one of them!'

'Here...what you found out then?'

'It says online that a body was found in an alleyway last Sunday morning, and at first people avoided going in thinking it was a pisshead or a junkie!'

'They weren't wrong!'

'Come on, *really*?'

'Sorry. Just trying to lighten the mood.'

'Don't.'

'This is just how *I* deal with stuff, I'm not being a dick.'

'I know mate. This is how *I* do.'

'Alright you two - it says the police were called when he hadn't moved by eleven o'clock…'

'For fuck's sake!'

'…and they got close enough to find he'd been stabbed repeatedly in the stomach. It had been raining but there was residue of a lot of blood on the ground underneath the body.'

'All that time, and me and Cookie must have just left him when it happened as well' said Hughesy, holding back a deep breath.

'It took a few days to identify him, it says. He wasn't wearing anything recognisable and didn't have a wallet on him. They knocked on doors but nobody was missing anyone.'

'Shit, man.'

'After the third day, it's got here that one of his neighbours contacted the police to say they knew who he was, and then his next of kin were informed. That'll be his Dad, aye?'

'Yeah, don't remember him ever having anyone else.'

'Poor bastard…imagine only having *that* in your life.'

'It's no wonder he was always pissed or stoned, is it?'

'It goes on, saying the father was informed and hadn't noticed Gaz hadn't been home…'

'For four *days*?'

'Apparently!'

'Wait, he lived with his Da still?'

'I never knew that! I just thought he'd got his own place.'

'Then it finishes saying date and time for the service, family and friends all welcome and that.'

'I can't believe it…'

'What's this moron slowing down for? Any more and we'll be reversing!'

'Erm...we're here lads.'

'Oh...right.'

'Pass me another couple of those bottles!'

-

Coming to a stop, everyone surged out of the truck cab before opening the back.

'Cheers, Dicky!'

'Aye, cheers for that!'

'I'm coming with you - pay my respects, yeah.'

'Yeah, course…'

'You lads been alright in the back?'

'We *may* owe you some money.'

'*You* mean *more* money, Bucky!'

'Back's killing; who buys a pick-up truck and has a big canopy over the back?'

'What you mean?'

'When you said some of us would need to go in the back I thought we'd be lounging in the sun, like, in a pick-up truck.'

'Yeah dude, that's not a comfortable place to be.'

'I don't normally carry eight blokes around the streets to be fair - and these lot nearly burst out of the cab!'

'Everyone ready to go in or what? It's ten past - we'll have to sneak in slowly so we don't disturb everyone.'

'Dicky gonna drive us in then?'

'Piss off!'

Lee reached the door first and slowly opened it just enough to pass through. Kev and Mitch did the same, before Knacker stepped up. Rolling his eyes, he pulled open both doors fully and walked in. The others followed, with Cookie bringing up the rear.

Beyond a small corridor adorned with artificial flowers in plastic vases on pine furniture, the room opened up to the right and around the corner. Cookie could hear someone talking, and silently edged behind the others to see the congregation.

There was none. Or, at least, barely one.

There were a total of fourteen people present. A policeman, in uniform, sat at the front with a woman sobbing quietly a foot or two along the pew to his left. A slim man in a black shirt and trousers sat on the opposite side, as far toward the wall as he could be. Sitting at the front of the room on a stool, almost festooned with yet more artificial flowers, was the priest, glaring at Kev. Almost as though he were levitating rather than using his feet, Kev slid gently behind Knacker.

Standing at the podium, visibly shaken and distraught, was a figure they had all known as children; withered and bleached. The folds around his eyes were closed, and he continued to speak through the throb of emotion.

'Is that…?'

'My son, my Gary, I've done *everything* for that boy and now he's gone…taken away…my little boy…'

'What a load of bollocks!'

'Shhh, Bucky - he's lost his son!'

'I don't buy it - horrible cu…'

'Shut it.' Cookie's hand covered Bucky's mouth.

'…I loved him with all my heart from the first time I ever laid eyes on him - my beautiful little…'

'Mmmm-mmmm'.
'Bucky's got a point', whispered Mitch.
'Will you shut the fuck up as well!'
The priest rose from his chair, and began to twitch his head in that way people do when they want someone to leave but it's not a good time to say that out loud.
'...I know that God will look after him now, and every night I pray...'
'Only God he's praying to is the God of whiskey!'
'Fucking hell, will you all just be quiet?' hissed Hughesy.
The priest began to move swiftly and silently toward the back of the room where they stood, between the two sets of pews. The slim man turned slightly to see where he was going, but quickly averted his eyes back to the front. The policeman heard only the sobbing of the woman, but glanced at the priest in confusion as he whisked by.
'...if only I could see him one more time, to tell him like I always did how proud I was of him...'
'You. All of you. Get out!', rasped the priest.
'We're here for our mate, to pay our respects!' whispered Kev.
'Some respect...look at the way you're all dressed for a sombre occasion...'Heaven is a what'?
'What?'
'Your t-shirt!'
'Oh, look, I know we got off on the wrong foot *last* time, but...'
'*Last* time?'
'Yeah, when I was caught short outside, you know.'
'That was *you*!'
'I thought you knew, you were staring at me when I walked in!'
'I was staring at *him* coming into *our* chapel *eating*!'
'It was in the car door, sorry Dicky!', said Knacker.
'It's okay.'
'It is not! Now get *out*!' The priest was struggling to stay calm now, and Gaz's Dad was wrapping up his speech.
'...if I saw him one more time...'
'Leave, *all* of you!'

'Two minutes, pal, he's nearly done!'
'...I would just want to tell him...'
'*Pal*? Two minutes? Get out!'
'Penguin's gonna blow!'
'*Penguin*? Get out now you...'
'...from the bottom of my heart, that he will *always* be my...'
'FUCKING CUNT!'

Chapter 4: Wake

'Cannot *actually* believe I've been called a cunt twice in the last month by a man of the cloth!'

'He's got to know you *so* quickly.'

'Yeah, took me years to realise you were a c-word!'

'Cat?'

'Clown?'

'A caravan?'

'Very good - I'm still just trying not to swear so much, lads.'

'Can we all still swear?'

'Until the Tales From the Crypt cast try and hobble you, fill your boots!'

'Nice one, you fucknugget!'

'Within reason.'

'Just over a month since we were all *last* stood here, you know. Is this *really* happening?'

'Not sure', said Lee. 'I can't…'

'Oy! If you say that one more time…he said it so often on the way here that I was worried Mr. Chips would turn up for a big money round!'

'Can't *believe* you're making jokes.'

'We were the same with this clown in the back!'

'C-word!'

'Some people react differently don't they?'

'Is there a *right* way?'

'No, there's not. Some people try to make everyone laugh, some just completely break down, some try to hold it together…'

'I'll be honest, lads - that one's me right now!' interrupted Dave.

'Where's Gaz when you need someone to cop a feel of your shoulder when you're at your most vulnerable?'

'Haha turns out you're that *first* type of person!'

'How was that a few weeks ago? Sitting in that pub?'

'Listening to 'Things Can Only Get Better'!'

'D:Ream can get to fuck, the bullshitting twats!'

'How is it less than an hour since we found out about this?

'And we've already attended the funeral?'
'Some of it.'
'There's another type of reaction, by the way' said Bucky, 'that's anger!'
'I'm angry too but there's time for that - I think that was well out of order what you were saying in there!'
'Cookie, do you not remember what Gaz's old man was like?'
'I do!' added Mitch as they started walking.
'Yes, I do. I'm sure we all do, but that was a time for grief and respects. I don't know what's happened between them over the past twenty-odd years but maybe they sorted things out.'
'I could *never* forgive someone like that.'
'No, me neither, but despite what he was like when we were kids, that man had lost his son; suddenly, tragically - he's allowed to grieve as he says goodbye for the last time.'
'I suppose - it was just hearing those lies…'
'I know.'
'Guessing we're going in there?' asked Lee as they left the black iron gates of the crematorium and waited to cross the road.
'Seems like it's where we go every time we have to put on our own wake, doesn't it.'
'As if there's an '*every time*' - I never thought of there being a first time until recently!'

-

In the corner, the TV screen continued to show horse racing. The same tables were taken by the same people in the same seats in the same clothes drinking the same drinks and probably having the same conversations. The barmaid began to pour four pints of lager, the glasses lined up next to the pump, while simultaneously checking her hair in the gaps of mirror beyond the spirit bottles.
'They for us?'
'Yeah love, what else was it again, couple of cokes…'
'Bloody hell, we've got a *usual*!'
'I'll have a lager as well today, please.'
'Just a double vodka, pet.'

'Just?'
'And was there a…'
'Cookie walked in through the door last.
'…oh, a virgin sex on the beach!'
'Shouldn't that be called a 'tricked on holiday by a bastard who never called'?
'Bit lengthy'.
'No, I'll have a pint of water please.'
'Can you stick the music channels on?'
'Sorry no - this lot *love* the racing.'

Not a single eye was focused on the telly. The lads began to sit down around the same two tables, pushed together, as they had before. Automatically, they took up the same positions and places around the table.

'You've left a pint here!'
'Shit…'
'I didn't even think.'
'Here you go', she said, as she set the remaining drink down on the mat in front of the empty chair. 'He at the loo?'
'No, he's over the road.'
'Thanks, love.'

Dave began to cry. At first, as he stared at the Gazless pint, his eyes filled up and then overflowed onto his cheeks. His shoulders began to shake, and then his whole body. When Dicky asked if he was okay the emotion burst out of him in a primeval yawn, causing everyone in the pub to turn and look at them. Sat next to Dave, Hughesy put his arm around his shoulder and pulled him in tightly.

Mitch hadn't felt it coming. It wasn't like slowly building waves, and there were no tears or shudders of warning, but from nowhere he burst into tears. Next to him, Kev was already leaning forward onto his hands, palms pressed firmly into his eyes, but motionless.

Contagiously, Lee and Bucky began to cry; all of them except Dicky and Cookie sobbed and made the noises children make when they're hurt but trying to tell you about it - those gasping intakes of breath and random syllables.

'Does anyone mind if I put the music channels on?' shouted the barmaid. 'No? There you go lads! It's alright now!'

By the time the final 'la la' of 'The Day We Caught The Train' faded out, apart from a few red faces, everyone had slipped back on the mask of masculinity and were trying to avoid each other's eyes. Dicky broke the silence.

'Sorry lads, I didn't know Gaz as well as you lot - I didn't even know his name was Gary, I thought it was Gareth - and I think I'm intruding a bit. Besides, I've got to make up the time on deliveries now.'

'You don't have to go mate.'

'I do - I'll have to get my foot down anyway - I can come back later when I'm done if you want picking up?'

'And get squashed in the back of your not-a-pick-up-truck?'

'And get driven around like we're on an over-eighties sightseeing tour?'

'By the Dukes of Spazzard!'

Smiles crept back onto the faces, and Dicky shook hands or hugged each of them before leaving, taking the extra time to squeeze Bucky's arm while holding his hand.

'Well', gasped Lee, 'that was *different*'.

'What must we have looked like, eh? All sat sobbing!'

'What must she think - we're emotionally attached to nineties pop songs, or we are dead set against horse racing?'

'I didn't cry.'

'Did you not?'

'I wanted to. You all were and seeing that empty chair and full f-bloody glass...but I couldn't.'

'What do you mean, we were?' smiled Dave. 'As if!'

'Why couldn't you then, big man?'

'I just...what?'

'Yeah, Lee, what's '*big man*' all about?'

'It just felt like a 'big man' type of moment; if this was an American sitcom someone would have said 'it's alright big guy.'

'Okay, but it isn't.'
'It's an English shitcom!'
'Alright, alright...why couldn't you then, wanker?'
'That's better!'
'I never show emotion, like that type of emotion, in public. I never have. When you look like this I suppose you're expected to act a certain way, be a *certain* type of man, that make sense?'
'Yeah, but it sounds awfully sad!'
'I love a good cry, me. Michael Keaton, My Life, makes me cry seven times every single time I watch it! I stick it on whenever I fancy a purge.'
'I'm the same as Bucky - What Dreams May Come for me, though!'
'Saw gets me!'
'Saw?'
'Aye - he's doing it all because of the death of his unborn kid at the hands of a junkie - completely heartbreaking!'
'I've never cried at a horror movie.'
'It's not horror - it's a man acting out real life vengeances, isn't it - it's a thriller. BUT if you were going to cry at a horror then it's *got* to be Friday The 13th!'
'Why?'
'Jason, man - feel *so* much sympathy for him!'
'Dude, are you telling us *you're* a serial killer?'
'No, he's tortured by his peers isn't he. I mean, he goes a bit over the top in his revenge…'
'A bit? He kills hundreds of people!'
'No, no - it's only about 165.'
'Oh well, fair play then.'
'So do you never let anyone see you emotional, big boy?'
'That's *not* what I said, you're making me sound creepy now!'
'No, never have. In the eighties growing up I think men were meant to act a certain way and my Dad instilled that in me. As we've got older people see me as the 'big man' and don't *want* to see that facade break.'
'That sounds tough.'

'I was with a lass, we'd been sleeping together a few times over the months, and I went for a shower.'

'Minger, was she?'

'It was the next morning. I'm in the shower and she shouts through that I've got a text, 'have you heard about Foz?' I told her to reply 'what's he done now?' and continued to wash.'

'Oh fucking hell - that was to *me*!', said Lee.

'So I'm…'

'Washing your hair?'

'No hair anywhere on me, mate!'

'Too much information.'

'I'm whistling some tune and she comes in the room, face like a ghost, and asks 'Who was Foz?' I'm in the middle of saying something about best mates when I realise what she's said. *Was*. Tiny word. This happy tune I've been whistling is still in my head when my legs just went underneath me and I'm crouched in the bottom of the shower cubicle, still with the shower on, naked and sobbing like I've *never* known before. She's dressed for work and is stuck on the other side of the glass not knowing what to do or say. I'm not built to do anything but stand upright in a shower so there's bits of me pressed up against the sides and she's watching what I can only imagine looks like a giant wet baby Houdini trying to escape a watery cell.'

'Mate…'

''Then I just felt angry - at Foz, at me for acting like that, at her for seeing it. I was pretty blunt, I think. She kept asking if I was okay, and I said I'd give her a call *sometime*. She had to get to work so that was that.'

'So you don't want to get emotional *again*? Is that what you're saying?'

'I'm saying I don't think I could no matter what. That's the only time I've been stripped bare in front of someone…'

'Emotionally!'

'Obviously - and it ruined something that might have become something else.'

'You were *finally* thinking of settling down then?

'No, well yeah, maybe - I don't know. Thing is, what's she going to think of me now?'

'That you're human?'

'She'd be way off!'

'Funny, but yeah -'

'So, have you not heard from her since?'

'No. I was pretty aggy, lads. It was the embarrassment. The shame.'

'No shame in crying, dude.'

'Possibly a bit of shame in crying with your dick pushed up against the glass, like a rogue butcher's window sausage!'

'The tip looking like that face we used to pull out the back of the bus, when you would fish hook both sides of your mouth and blow against the glass!'

'Haha'.

'How it took this long for a pandemic, beyond me!'

'So you know, *you* don't have to hide emotions around *us*, Cookie.'

'Yeah mate - we're all here for each other...we all need to vent and get support at times, you know.'

'We might take the piss, but it's equal opportunities mockery here!'

'Yeah, whether you're a giant or a homeless or a gay - everyone gets the same treatment.'

'I'll bear that in mind. Thank you, lads. Seriously.'

'No bother.'

'Big boy.'

Chapter 5: Taxi

'*Closing time...you don't have to go home but you can't stay here...*'

'How did it get to closing time?'

'Why am I cold?'

'We're *outside*!'

'*Closing time...you don't have to go home but you can't stay here...*'

'Someone ringing a taxi?'

'Why are I is *outside*?'

'I need a wee!'

'*Closing time...you don't have to go home but you can't stay here...*'

'Is that the only line you three know?'

'Erm...yeah.'

'I'm nipping for a slash!'

'Where have the walls gone?'

'We're *outside*, man!'

'I've booked two taxis, they didn't have a minibus available. They'll be five minutes.'

'Charlatans?'

'Who is?'

'No, I think it's a real taxi company!'

'Sang Closing Time!'

'No no no - Mitch, Lee and Bucky sang it!'

'I mean the *actual* song. The whole thing, not just one line.'

'Wasn't Charlatans…'

'Goo Goo Dolls?'

'Where's Hughesy?'

'Piss.'

'I'm joining him!'

'Quick, taxi be two minutes!'

'*Closing time...you don't have to go home but you can't stay here...*'

'Barenaked Ladies?'

'Where?'

'No, man - sang the song!'

'Naw, they sang One Week!'
'What's happening in a week?'
'One of us is probably gonna die!'
'Shit, Dave...'
'Fucking hell - '
'Sorry, lads. Don't know where *that* came from.'

Lights illuminated the front of the pub, and the six figures staggering, leaning or singing in front of it.

'Taxi! Who's in the first one?'

They then drifted past, and the car turned along the side of the pub, illuminating the backs of Hughesy and Bucky as they stood facing the wall.

'Not a taxi, dudes.'
'Ah, we're not doing anything wrong are we!'
'Think those two are.'

The doors opened and two policemen exited the car, leaving the headlights directed at the two backs.

'Right then, gentlemen, that's enough', said the first.
'Erm...what, sorry?'
'It's a crime to urinate in public.'
'We aren't unirating!'
'Oh, so what are you doing?'
'We've been told off, that big one's our *Dad* and the fat one's our *Mam*. We have to face the wall!'
'Very good. Let's turn around *now*, shall we?'
'We're not doing a weewee!'
'Mate, a fucking *weewee*?'
'If that were the case, can you explain why you are exposing your bare behind to the world?'

Hughesy leaned back and looked at Bucky's arse. 'Why the hell have you got your pants down?'

'Having a wee mate, but don't tell Officer Dibble!'
'Turn around, now. *Both of you*!'

Bucky began to turn to his right while Hughesy began to turn to his left.

'Fellas, turn the other way!'
'Ah, don't cross the streams, Egon!'
'I take it you're both drunk?'
'You take it?'

'We don't even know you but I'm glad you feel comfortable sharing…'

'What on earth happened to your arm?'

'It's a long stor…'

'Oh, it's you lot *again*! Why am I not surprised?'

'Do we know you?'

'I do - hello again. Yeah so the arm hasn't been healing very well!'

'Did you go straight to the hospital once the fire brigade had safely removed the door?'

'Ah - no, no I didn't.'

'Well, I suppose that's karma right there!'

'Yeah!'

'You should go and get that checked out, Mr. Buck!'

'Aye, aye, I will.'

'Look, I know why you're out together, *again*, and there's nobody around so please, just be on your way.'

'We've booked a taxi!'

'There's two groups of *four* this time, by the way; there's not eight of us together!'

'That restriction was lifted.'

'Oh, right. Good.'

The officer walked toward the front of the building, and addressed everyone. 'All of you, please keep the noise down and no more public urinating until your taxi has arrived.'

'We're not making noise, Brigadier!'

'Brigadier? That's a copper!'

'Oh I thought we were on a ship!'

How much has Kev had?'

'Listen, we've heard someone singing the whole time we've been here - just heed advice and keep it down!'

As the policemen were getting back into their car, Mitch shouted 'Here, who sang Closing Time?'

'Ash! Now go home, all of you!'

-

'Have you rang them?'

'Yeah, they said it's just 'round the corner!'

'Why is it every taxi is always just around the corner?'

'Same as every pizza delivery!'

'Alright, Knacker, don't get aroused.'

'Hope that driver can cope with those lot.'

'They were canny mortalled like.'

'Do you reckon we can ask Dicky to come back for us still?

'It's nearly midnight - I think he meant *before* teatime.'

'Selfish twat!'

'He probably wouldn't wanna get Knacker again anyway...'

'Oh haha because I broke his suspension guffaw guffaw *very* funny!'

'Well, I meant because you stole his dinner!'

'Oh!'

'I forgot about that - who wanders into a funeral eating a pasta pot?'

'I ordered food at the bar before I came around, but then we rushed out didn't we.'

'Well I forgot to go to the cashpoint so I'll just steal someone's wallet, yeah?'

'When you put it like that!'

'Car!'

'Right, see you all soon then?'

'You not getting in Hughesy?'

'I just live up the road a bit - opposite direction for the rest of you.'

'We don't mind!'

'It's fine...'

'Why have you waited all this time with us?'

'Just wanted to be with you lads - and to let the coppers have chance to get out of the area.'

'Half expected you to pull Gaz out of your pocket!'

'Right, well yeah we will see you soon.'

'Later, mate.'

'Bye, lads!'

Lee, Cookie and Knacker got into the taxi, which illuminated Hughesy for a moment as it pulled around in a circle and began to head in the opposite direction, away from the pub and the crematorium. Before Hughesy disappeared from sight, someone had already asked 'Been busy tonight, like, pal?'

Chapter 6: Group Chat

Tuesday

Dave
Twats! Is that how I'm supposed to start a group message? I'm on the Facebook. Wondering if you would all be up for a third attempt at meeting up. Third time lucky! Not in a bar.
I was thinking Costa, 11am next Saturday?

Lee
I'm up for that. We've got a lot to talk about.

Mitch
Firstly, we need to discuss Dave joining the industrial revolution

Cookie
Yeah I need to see you lot anyway - got some news

Dave
Well, I've been trying to tell you all something for ages, so I'm looking forward to just getting together.

Bucky
I'm barred from Costa. What about the Early Learning Centre?

Hughesy
Few things to ask, but main one is why the Early Learning Centre?

Bucky
It has tables and chairs.

Hughesy
Like the pubs and cafs do?

Bucky
Dave said no pubs. I'm barred from all the cafs in town.

Dave
We can do a pub if you want!

Bucky
I'm barred from all the pubs as well.

Kev
Bloody hell

Bucky
It was, yeah!

Dave
What about the other day?
Bucky
Why i wore the hat
Cookie
Master of disguise, you mate
Mitch
There's loads of picnic areas in the park. Been taking Marie's kids.
Kev
Lee better not wear his paedo pants if we're going to a park.
Lee
I'll wear you!

Wednesday

Dave
Which park?
Mitch
West Park - main entrance then swing a left
Dicky
THE facebook?
Bucky
Who added you?
Dicky
Dave must have, when he was setting up the group on THE facebook using the world wide web
Knacker
I'll be there lads
Be like a school outing
Dave
Excellent. West Park, next saturday, 11am. Over.
Lee
Okay Rubber Duck, see you then.
Bucky
Ten-four good buddy

Chapter 7: Outing

The sun shone dazzlingly onto the park, brighter and hotter than usual geographically. Ringed by a red, wrought iron fence, the area was a couple of acres of peace in an otherwise built-up industrial town. To the right of the main entrance, a couple of hundred feet along a nonsensically winding path which could have gone straight, was the play area: swings, slide, roundabout, fag ends, probable essential tetanus injections.

To the left of the entrance was a vast expanse of green where families sat on blankets, children wobbled on their first bike rides, and sticks were thrown for happy dogs. As if trying to make the scene postcard-perfect, a man and his wife played frisbee with their two daughters, who had clearly never experienced the prehistoric fun of a flying disc.

Along a line of trees at the far side of the field were positioned several picnic benches, two of which were taken up by a group of men in their late thirties. Three sat on each bench, with their feet on the seats, facing each other, and one was stood between the two.

'Just Cookie and Knacker we're waiting on, but I really wanted to speak to you *all*.'

'Same', said Lee. 'I know it's meant to be a running joke now but I am really struggling to get my head...I'm *struggling*! I've started getting hypnosis!'

'You're a chicken!', shouted Bucky.

'What?'

'I don't mean like scared, I just thought I'd see if you acted like a chicken!'

'It's not that kind of hypnosis mate.'

'You're an aeroplane!'

'No.'

'Will you shut up and let him speak?'

'He said he's been hypnotised!'

'It's really helping with relaxing; '*calming the mind*' they call it.'

'Calming the bank manager - it's all bullshit that stuff, man!'

'I'm telling you it isn't - each to their own and that but it's *definitely* working for me!'
'How much?'
'Not much, just £60 a session.'
'Fucking hell, nee wonder you need calming!'
'Never mind, lads…'
'Lee?'
'Yeah.'
'Are you okay?'
'Yeah, I'm just struggling to sleep and can't deal with them both being gone.'
'There's people you can talk to…'
'Like him thinking I'm going to strut around like farm animals?'
'No, I mean there's actual human people. Since we were out for Foz I've popped in to see his Ma a couple of times, and there's a company, like a charity, trying to help her out.'
'I don't need that sort of help, mate.'
'Okay, but you know where I am, *right*!'
'Yeah, I mean thank you, as well. I appreciate it.'
'Don't get bent, you two!'
'On that subject, what *I* wanted to talk…' interjected Dave, who had been waiting to speak for some time.
'Here's the Knacker, now!'
'Where've you been, mate?'
'You said go left at the swings so I've been wandering around the play park for twenty minutes looking like a lunatic.'
'Nobody said that mate.'
'You did, in the chat. Anyway I'd completely forgotten about that place but there was a proper dangerous roundabout there back in the day. I flew off it when I was about 7 and broke my leg, you remember when I was off Primary ages?'
'Oh yeah, and you came back fat!'
'Well, I had to sit still for months, felt like years, and the parents were working so me Gran watched me and just fed me all day watching Fifteen-To-One and that!'

'*She's* to blame, then? Not the subsequent three decades of gorging?'

'Damn right, Knacker - the old bitch!.'

'Anyway, that's all changing now.'

'Really? Is McDonald's closing down?'

'No, it turns out I've got diabetes. Strict orders to sort myself out!'

'So, McDonald's is going to go bust instead?'

'Think of all those young people who failed their GCSEs...what will *they* do now you selfish prick?'

'Lads…' said Dave.

'I lost my fucking *teeth* on that roundabout, you know! Shame that isn't what happened to you, Knacker, eh?'

'How did you lose your teeth?'

'That must have been some spin!'

'Not off the speed, ya wally!'

'No. So the one Knacker's on about was made of splintered old wood, and was lots of panels nailed together rather than a piece of metal. Each panel had like a beam joining it to the centre and the next panel underneath.'

'Alright, beautiful mind…'

'I know this because I was on it one day and these other kids got on, a *lot* bigger than me. Their Da comes over, starts spinning it and they're all laughing, but I'm not because I can feel my grip sliding away. When I'm at the opposite side to the bloke I kind of slipped off but didn't fly through the air like Knacker, I dropped straight down and these beams came one after the other, at such speed, and smashed into my head. I remember a few of them, then waking up with my Ma screaming over me and I had no teeth at all at the front - top *or* bottom.'

'Oh mate, I remember that! We called you Gummi Bears for ages!'

'Yeah, cheers, whenever I came into school I'd hear '*bouncing here and there and everywheeeeere*!'

'A classic song that we could have easily sang for Knacker *as well*!'

'Right, lads, *listen*...oh, here's Cookie coming over, I'll wait until he gets here' said Dave.

'What's up with you, Mitch?'
'Huh?'
'You're quiet!'
'Oh just shattered - I've started staying over at Marie's and I'm not used to getting woken up *three times* during the night.'
'I'd *love* that - I make do with a monthly if I'm lucky, with a bonus birthday bang!'
'Interesting but not shagging - I wish! The kids are always up during the night!'
'Mammy, why's that flasher *still* in our house?'
'Mammy, that man with the angry purple ferret is in your bed!'
'No, it's more like 'mammy, I'm just coming in to be a shithead and remind you that we are your kids and we control *everyfuckingthing* in your life!'
'That sounds wonderful!'
'Cookie mate, Mitch is just lamenting the fact that the kids he traumatised can't sleep now.'
'Sorry I'm late, I've been dealing with some stuff that I really need your help with.'
'Actually, I've been waiting for you to get here to *finally* tell everyone…' said Dave, before being cut off.
'I'm pregnant!'
'Don't think *you* are.'
'If Knacker said that, we'd possibly believe it possible!'
'Knob!'
'Haha no I mean I'm having a baby, a woman is having a baby, a woman is having *my* baby that I threw up inside her!'
'And that's sex education finished for today class.'
'I didn't know you were seeing anyone mate, you never said the day of Gaz's...you know.'
'Yeah you were just on about squeaking your tail around some bird's bathroom.'
'Well, yeah, I said we'd been seeing each other for a while…'
'Thought you always *'jizz* on the *tits'* as you so eloquently put it?'

'Well, that's worked until now. I think I said it could have been more but I ruined it, we had started getting more serious and it was far beyond just shagging.'

'Lads…'

'Did she just get in touch then?'

'No, I sent her some appalling apologetic messages after I got home last time. Wasn't even drunk, just all these emotions came flooding out. I told her I'd been drunk, *obviously*!'

'Obviously, yeah!'

'So we met up this morning for a walk down the beach, and I asked her for another chance…'

Lads, sorry Cookie but…'

'…and she's just *so* happy and *then* she tells me…'

'I'M GAY!' Suddenly Dave flew to his feet, enraged, arms flailing. 'I'm gay! I'm fucking gay! I'm a homo! A knob jockey! A faggot, a fairy and a fudge packer! I am a friend of Dorothy, a nancy, a pansy, a poof, an arse bandit, a fucking batty boy!

'Dave!'

'I'm a bender, fairy, meat masseuse, bone smuggler, bum boy, cockpipe cosmonaut! A donut puncher, a crafty butcher, a turd burglar, a ring raider, a sperm gurgler, a woolly woofter, a shirt lifter…'

'*Dave* mate…'

'…a pillow biting cockstruction worker, a marmite miner, a Queen from Oklahomo, an Elton, a limpwrist, a mary, a fucking queer…'

'We *know* you're gay!'

'…I'm a...what?'

'Yeah dude, we all know you're gay.'

'Bloomin' good list though!'

'Well, I've been called them all - what do you mean, you all know?'

'Is *that* what you wanted to tell us?'

'What's next? Breaking news, Kev is a homeless Aids-riddled anorexic?'

'Shock horror!'

'Exclusive! Read all about it!'

'I don't know what to say, lads. How *long* have you all known?'

'I'd say sorry to the frisbee family over there first!'

'Oh...sorry about all that!'

Angrily, with the father holding the youngest in his arms and the mother covering the oldest's ears, they stormed away across the field toward the play park.

'Since school, mate.'

'*School*?'

'Yeah, we were at Mitch's when I realised!'

'Watching that awful seventies porn?'

'Oh *yeah*...what was it called again?'

'Pee Fun Lovers!', announced Mitch, proudly.

There wasn't any sex though, from what I remember.'

'I'm gonna admit right now lads', added Hughesy, 'I was there in the room so I could be one of the lads, but I was holding in a vom!'

'What was happening in this film, like?' asked Dicky, stepping from the trees.

'Dicky, completely forgot you were in the group.'

'Just got here, went left at the swings then realised the message had said 'swing *a* left'.

'They were just pissing on each other mate!'

'Fuck off!'

'Serious - we'd all been convinced to go 'round...'

'We *were* only about 13!'

'...to watch *porn*, and you'd see more up against the side of the VG!'

'I lost that video *and* got bollocked off me Da!'

'It's lovely to reminisce...'

'Men in piss!'

'...but how did that tell you all *I* was gay?'

'Because afterward whenever we mentioned it *you* mentioned the cocks!'

'Haha did I?'

'Yeah, we all talked about it, I think, didn't we lads, at different times?'

'Yeah, mate. You'd always be taking the piss, saying stuff like 'even his cock looked sad', or...'

'It was so seventies his willy had sideburns!'
'...yeah, that *was* pretty funny actually, but the rest of us never mentioned the dick!'
'I didn't even notice the penises, there were tits on show!'
'Aye, covered in piss!'
'Cover it in cow shit it's still a boob and I'm still looking!'
'I've tried telling you all *so* many times, but just couldn't.'
'You never *needed* to mate.'
'But you shouldn't have ever been scared to tell your mates who you are.'
'Unless you're a serial killer.'
'Like the Jason-sympathiser over there!'
'I wasn't *not* telling you because of *you*, it was because of me!'
'I tried to get you to admit it the other week, when we were saying goodbye mate!'
'When you called me a homophobe?'
'Yeah, what's that all about then?'
'I really tried to overcompensate and hide it when I went to college and then to Uni - until I met my husban...why do you lot always ask after my *wife*?'
'See you squirm!'
'You didn't invite us to your wedding. We just thought we'd wait until you were ready to out yourself.'
'It was a really small service, my parents didn't want to come so we didn't really invite anyone. It was just Michael's parents, his sister and...'
'...Foz!'
'Yes. Lads, I'm going to be honest here I've waited thirty years to tell you all and you know *everything*, it's a bit weird. I don't know whether I'm happy or furious!'
'You're out *now*, we aren't bothered if you get angry; are you going to throw glitter at us or something?'
'Dick!'
'You're *obsessed*!'
'Well, how did you know about Foz?'
'How did Foz know and we didn't?'
'Yeah, answer *that* first!'
'It's a bit cringy, to be fair.'

'I had to tell you all about my big fella peeping out of my jeans the other week!'

'Okay...so I'm lying on me bed, I'm about fourteen, and I'm watching, you know, and having a hand shandy, then Foz walks in my bedroom.'

'Really built up that story mate!'

'Bloody hell, Tolkien, cut out some of the description will you!'

'Fuck off, it still pains me to just *think* about it!'

'What did he say?'

'The twat looked me up and down, looked at the telly, and said 'are you *coming*?'

'Hahahahaha Foz man...'

'I would have legged it out of your room!'

'Not many people would hang around and make a joke, like.'

'But how did that mean you were out out?'

'Because of what I was watching!'

'Which was?'

'Sorry mate...Pee Fun Lovers!'

'You fucking nicked it?'

'But you could have been looking at the boobies!'

'It was on pause!'

'Oh...'

'No way...'

'Yep, on a flaccid, sad willy with flares and a handlebar moustache!'

Chapter 8: Taking the Michael

'I still can't believe they've known all along!'

'Now I've had time to think about it, it's pretty cool. I was so worried about coming out to my friends and spoiling or ruining what they felt and thought about me, that it never occurred to me that they would feel exactly the same way no matter what.'

'Those who mind, don't matter and those who matter, don't mind!'

'Alright, Socrates!'

'I think it was Dr. Seuss actually!'

'I'm *really* looking forward to you meeting each other!'

'Same - I'm just trying to remember who's who. Cookie is a giant, Kev is homeless, Knacker - what's his real name, that sounds horrible - is overweight, Hughesy has long hair, Bucky has short hair and tattoos, Lee has receding hair...who've I missed?'

'Mitch!'

'Oh, right...Mitch looks...I don't know.'

'Tired.'

'He's in a new relationship, yes, you said.'

'A new *old* relationship!'

'She's called Marie, the one who lives near us that you often wave at!'

'That's the one.'

'And I'm assuming he looks tired because of all the…'

'Kids!'

'That they're busy making?'

'No, ready-made ones.'

'Ooh. Still, it's the way we'd have to go!'

'I'd rather have my lie-ins and holidays, and have you to myself!'

'But we've been together nearly twenty years - I'm bored of you - my homovaries aren't getting any younger, David!'

'You are going to fit in perfectly here, you know!'

Dave and Michael parked outside the working men's club, and walked around to the front door. A silver sign read 'Engagement Party Upstairs' and confetti had been strewn all over the steps leading up to the right. In a booth on the left, a vinegar-faced man somewhere between sixty and ninety sat and stared in disgust at the floor.

'Come for the party?'

'No, the dominoes, love', replied Michael.

'It's upstairs', came the apathetic reply.

At the top of the stairs, before the doors leading into the function room, Michael said he would just go to the toilet.

'Nervous?'

'No, I just don't want to have to leave the room and know people are calling me a bender during the night!'

'I'll head in.'

Unlike most engagement or wedding parties, or birthdays for that matter, everyone who had been invited had turned up. That was the way of the world in between lockdowns - get as much partying done as possible before the Spitting Image puppets announced another period being cooped up finding out how little you actually liked the people you thought you loved. For this reason, Dave was surprised that he spotted his group of lads instantly, and rushed over.

'Davey!'

'Where's the wusband?'

'Toilet!'

'Another George Michael?'

'No, and please take it easy on him. *He's* excited to finally meet you lot, but I've got that fear you get when you introduce your worlds to each other!'

'Never fear - we love queer!'

'Oh dear!'

'There you are - I couldn't see you anywhere!'

'Michael, *this* is the lads…'

'*And* lasses!'

'Oh, sorry, I didn't notice you there…'

'Because I was behind Knacker?'

'She's in there with the abuse, amazing!'

'Lads, Marie, this is Michael, my husband!'

'Hello, Michael, it is awfully nice to meet you!'

'A pleasure to make your acquaintance, Sir!'

'How do you do - '

'What *are* you all doing?'
'Being nice!'
'Don't, it doesn't suit you and he knows all about you!'
'Hope not!'
'I do actually - you're Cookie and you've just managed to formulate a relationship with a full human and not just a pair of breasts, you're Kev who doesn't shit himself anymore but looks like he smells like he does, Hughesy you have two kids who everyone says are terrifying but we have no idea why, Lee is a paedo, Bucky grabs cocks, Marie we've seen each other many times but it's nice to be introduced, this must be Mitch next to you who I'm grateful to say has his shirt untucked so I cannot see his waistline, Knacker you are not as ginormous as I expected!'
'The bender does know us!'
'Welcome, Mike!'
'Michael, please!'
'Mickey, lad, good to meet you! Does your dick have a tank top on?'
'Oh - it seems there are *some* things I have not been given research on!'
'Ask Dave about…'
'Anyway, lovely to see you all again', rushed Dave, 'for a positive occasion for once!'
'Yeah, I've been looking forward to this!'
'I'm gonna go find the lady, catch up in a bit', said Cookie.
'Dave said you'd been at the toilets, Mikey boy - is that a gay thing? You have to check the facilities on arrival?'
'No actually, it's a man thing that once you start drinking you have to go to the loo a lot - if you were one you'd know.'
'Oh Kev, he's done ya!'
'While I was there I *did* meet a man though…'
'Fast work!'
'…he offered me pills, then asked if I was police - surely he has his sales pitch back to front!'
'In here? The big club?'
'They get everywhere, the little urchins do!'
'Here you go, darling!'

Every eye at the table moved and fixed itself on Knacker's wife, including Dave, Michael and Marie's.

'Is it diet?'

'Yes, of course. Hi, Dave and Michael, yes? I'm *'Mountain's'* wife, I guess!'

'Mountain?'

'Mount Neverest!'

'Mount Heaviest!'

'Oh, that's better than mine!'

'Do you not call him *Mountain*?'

'No, *we* call him Knacker!'

'Thanks, lads!'

'Knacker? That's awful - like a testicle?'

Mitch interrupted, 'No, no - Knacker as in he would always stand up for his mates and *knack* anyone who messed with us, you know?'

'Oh...oh, ah that's *nice* babe! Why did you tell me they called you Mountain?'

'I erm...didn't want you thinking I was aggressive or anything!'

'No, I think it's *very* sexy! *Very* protective!'

'What's happening?', asked Bucky, returning from the bar.

'Knacker's missus was just asking about him being called 'Mountain' mate.'

'Mountain? Aye, Mount Killamanforajarofnutella!'

'That's better than mine as well! Neverest sounded good in *my* head!'

'So Mickster', asked Lee, 'what do you do?'

'Apart from *men*, you mean?'

'Do you not mind making gay jokes?', asked Marie.

'Humour is always how minority groups deal with society, isn't it. Different races, genders, orientations, gingers - there will always be people get offended on behalf of certain groups, but if you're no longer having us hanged for our natural inclinations then say what you want, in my view. Nothing was ever mended by being offended, only by standing up and doing something. If it's *completely* off the table to joke about, doesn't that mean we aren't having the open, frank discussions we should be having? That we're hiding from it, whatever *it* is. That as a society we've gone from demonising something to *victimising* it?'

'That was a bit deep!'

'Dave said that last night!'

'Wahey!'

'I like you, Mick!'

'It's Michael!'

'Sorry, Mikey-boy!'

'I had this discussion with Foz once, years and years ago when I first met him through Dave, and he made a joke, don't even remember what it was but it was at Dave's expense for being gay. I got my back up and had a go at him, in front of *loads* of people in the Uni bar and they all clapped when I was done.'

'Good for you.'

'No, it wasn't - because God rest his soul that boy was a bastard and was *always* right!'

'How come?'

'He sat there, didn't flinch or retaliate or anything as I shouted in his face about *being* homophobic and *not being* a good friend and all this crap that I thought sounded good. Then he sips off his pint and gets up, Dave looks at me like I should apologise and I look back like I've won, not realising I've *already* lost! He walks straight over to the karaoke, it's between singers and he just takes the mic and taps it.'

'I knew Michael was about to fall in love right there and then…'

'Everyone looks over at this *'homophobe'* who's just been put in his place, and he says 'If I didn't take the piss out of my friend for being a gayboy then I'd not be a friend. How many of you stuck-up little shitballs would call someone spotty 'spotty', or short 'short', or ugly 'ugly' behind their back? That's superficial shit that isn't even who that person is *inside*, and you'd not be honest with them. Just don't fucking say it. Be kind. Be nice. Be a dick to your mates about the stuff they think *is* important to let them know that it isn't. It isn't off limits or sacred or some shit because then you'd be saying 'that thing about you, that's different'. Difference shouldn't be about being 'other'. I call my fat mate 'fat', and my massive mate 'giant' and my skinny runt mate 'homeless' and my thick mate 'spaz' which I admit is a tad harsh, and if I didn't call my Dave 'gay' when he is fucking gay, for fuck's sake, then I would be being different with him BECAUSE of his benderness! *That* would be fucked up. *That* would be queer!'

'Foz lad!'

'The place didn't give him a little clap either, did it Michael?'

'Did it hell, place erupted and they all started chanting 'gay' at Dave. Think a lot of them, studying law or politics or something, probably felt bad about that the next day but the sentiment was a good one at the time, I guess.'

'He then sang 'What's Up' but changed all of the 'hey-ay-ay-ayay' bits to 'gay-gay-gay-gayay', and Michael *was* in love.

'So you were close to Foz a long time then?'

'Yeah Mick, we would often see his pictures had you and Dave in them!'

'Nearly twenty years, I guess. After that night, I saw him for what *he* was: an absolute beauty of a twat!'

'Surprised you'd know what one of *those* looked like!'

'Oh I've seen pictures. Not like Dave who dipped his wick to 'be straight'.

'Alright then, let's change the subject, eh?'

'Mitch is moving in with me, so he's going to be just around the corner from you two!'

'Nice one, Marie - I don't mean to sound rude, and tell me if it's none of my business…'

'It's none of *your* business!'

'But isn't that a bit quick?', asked Lee.

'I've got Lee's back here; I thought the same. What is it, two months since you rekindled with Knacker watching?'

'You did what?'

'He's exaggerating, love! I didn't see *anything*!'

'It feels like we've *always* been together I think - that's why we seem to be moving so fast.'

'Yeah, it's like there hasn't been twenty-odd years between us - he's *amazing* with the kids as well...they love him!'

'We heard he's been entertaining them with balloon animals!'

'Have you?'

'Bucky's just being a moron - it's as though there hasn't been twenty-odd years of maturity between his ears!', growled Mitch.

'Well, you're still not moving as quickly as *these* two!', said Lee as everyone else in the room went completely silent and the music stopped.

Hughesy ducked behind his own hand as all eyes turned toward Lee sat next to him.

'I didn't say it was a *bad* thing!'

'Ahem...are we good, can you hear? Good, right. Well, apart from Lee, who is a raging paedo by the way, thank you all for coming. All the gifts, we can't believe it, you're all so generous! Obviously I want to say I love this woman, and we cannot wait to get married, but seeing how many of you have turned out is a bit worrying for the length of the guest list and we may have to have a secret wedding on a beach somewhere. *Joking*, Nana! Anyway, thank you, the buffet's open and you'd better get there before my mate *Mountain*, and enjoy the rest of the night. Thank you all for coming. *Except* Lee.'

Everyone clapped and then one by one, all stared at Lee again.

'He's *joking*, man!'

'Mrs Knacker? Who's got the kids tonight?'

'What? Oh, their grandparents. *Knacker* here has been quite a changed man since your night out for Foz. He's *insisted* we get out and do things together. Really forceful in a sexy way.'

'One night in tight Lycra was it all it took to reset his balls by the sounds of it!'

'Want any speed?'

'Sorry?'

'Speed? Got coke. Sniff! Spliffs? Couple pills?'

'Fuck off, pal!'

'Woah, Mitch! What are *you* doing here? Marie? Am I in the past?'

'Do we know you?'

'Leave them alone and move on mate, right!'

'Bucky! Wait, all of you, this is trippy as fuck, man!

'Is that *you*, Hedz?'

'Yes, it is me! I've come from the future to tell you something but I don't know what it is!'

'We're in the present dude!'

'Maybe', said Michael, 'it's to warn us there's a junky selling drugs in the toilets?'

'Maybe it *is* to warn you there's a junky selling drugs in the toilets! I've been in there all night and I haven't seen him - I'll go and check!'

'No Hedz lad, he's messing with you. What on earth are you doing?'

'I'm a businessman, past Hughesy - but I'm trying to avoid that po-po over there!'

'What's a po-po?'

'A Teletubby with a stutter I reckon!'

'It's police - you gotta talk like the kids, man!'

'We *are* the kids, it's 1995 mate, school disco!', said Mitch.

'Now you're being silly!'

'*Really*?'

'School discos were at the community centre, *not* the big club!'

'Oh that's the illogical part?'

'Do you want some ketamine? Or glue?'

'No man, we're grown-ups at our mate's engagement do...why would *we* want to get high?'

'Hedz love, do you want to just sit down with us for a bit?', asked Marie.

'Gentlemen!'

Just as his bum touched the gaudily-patterned seating, the word sent him fleeing from the table and into the crowd of revellers.

'*And* ladies, thank you!'

'Sorry, I'm used to seeing this lot in an all-male ensemble!'

'Who are you?'
'Bucky, it's the copper -'
'Can I sit down?'
'What copper?'
'The one we repeatedly have run-ins with!'
'He was with *you* at Dicky's house, caught *you* pissing against the pub the other week...'
'Oh, don't recognise you pal!'
'He's not wearing a uniform...'
'But I have *exactly* the same face. Is he always drunk?'
'No, just when we're together!'
'Which is becoming more frequent!'
'After dealing with this one's idiocy I was called to an old couple who had been saved from a bag of burning dog poo, to a house where paramedics had removed a 'dying sporty Jesus' from a door, then to a family who said a fat man ran through their fence, then to a lady who claimed someone had just stolen her son's ashes, before...'
'Can I just say it wasn't dog...'
'It wasn't us! Is what he's *trying* to say.'
'As well as two calls from the Happy Shopper staff, one early on to say there was a fight outside, and one just around closing time telling us they were worried about locking up as *someone* was banging on the doors! All of this happened when you lot were back in town, wandering the streets and acting like teenagers!'
'We didn't *steal* any ashes - I went in to see Foz's Ma, that's our mate who died...'
'I know. I've been there a lot recently, since she lost her husband she's often been ringing...at first we thought she was wasting our time, making things up, you know...'
'Bloody hell!'
'Then her son is gone and it escalates. Keeps reporting him missing!'
'Some might say it's a positive, that she can't remember they've died?'
'They'd be idiots, wouldn't they! They wouldn't be the ones having to console the poor woman at three in the

morning because her husband has been abducted, or her son is in the attic but won't answer her.'

'Bloody hell!'

'Then the next day, anyway, we were called to your friend, Gary.'

'*You* found Gaz?'

'Yeah...that sort of thing doesn't happen around here. I told Buck here that it's a quiet place, that nothing ever happens, but that changed a lot afterward.'

Hedz ran past behind the officer, shouting 'I'll be back...from the future!'

'Look, I'm not on duty - I'm here because my wife is cousins with the lass getting engaged, but seeing you all here I had to come and ask...was there anyone might have had anything against him?'

'Gaz was lush mate, wouldn't ever hurt anyone, always the one who got a crack when it was *never* his fault!'

'We *were* involved in the altercation at the VG earlier in the night, but I think he was in the shop at the time, wasn't he?'

'Yeah, he wasn't involved - in fact they'd gone before he even came out.'

'Okay, but what do you know about them?'

'They started on Knacker here...'

'Did they? Is that where you got that black eye, my love?'

'I didn't want to worry you...yeah there were two brothers, and there was a big lad called Sean...'

'..and a young lass, real little Terrahawk!', added Lee.

'I think I might know who you mean, often around the shop. Haven't heard it called the VG for a long time, since I was a kid!'

'And there's his Dad!'

'What?'

'Gaz's Dad - real piece of work - *always* beating Gaz up when we were kids, proper vicious.'

'He wouldn't kill his *own son*', Marie said, half as a statement, half a question.

'He tried often enough back in the day! Gaz was always covered in bruises, bandaged or in plaster, saying how he'd barricaded himself in his room and that!'

'Well that's *not* how he came across at the funeral, or when we've spoken to him and to others who knew them both.'

'That was *you* at the crem?'

'Yeah - it became apparent *quickly* that there wouldn't be many mourners, nobody had been in touch with the family...I felt it proper that someone was there to pay respects. I heard the pastor shouting and saw you all leaving, but hadn't heard you come in.'

'We don't need *roads'*, screeched Hedz again as he ran back the other way. The officer turned slightly to look but he was already out on the stairway by the toilets again.

'I pulled over that night to speak to you all, but got distracted by these two urinating in public; I said I knew why you were all out together - that's why I let you off because I know what you must be going through, I just don't want your reactions to be something stupid *again*.'

'No, no, we're not going to be getting drunk on the streets and smashing the town up again mate. Promise. We just got a little out of hand.'

'Or a little out of *arm*, in my case', grinned Bucky.

'Sorry to have intruded...I will look into this more but at the minute there's so little to go on. At first we thought it had been a mugging gone wrong, but once we finally identified Gary and visited his house, his wallet and watch and everything were there.'

'Was his phone there?'

'Erm...no we never recovered a phone.'

'Cheers.'

'His father said his phone had been broken - didn't know where it was. Did he have a phone with him on that Saturday night?'

'Don't know actually, he just kept saying it wasn't working.'

'Okay, ring the station if you think of anything else.'

'Yeah, sure thing...and don't worry, we won't do *anything* stupid!', promised Dave.

'What did *he* want?', asked Cookie, returning to the table.

'Asking about Gaz, among others.'

'Any craic?'

'Well, he did say that group of rats *always* hangs around the VG!'

'And that Gaz's phone wasn't recovered!'

'Right. I've got to keep up the gracious host bollocks with Sarah, but I'll be at the VG next Friday and Saturday from six - *six*, Knacker!'

'We might be doing *something* stupid after all!'

Chapter 9: Bet

'I bet you get in trouble she said, she's *really* not happy, thinks we're being ridiculous.'

'Knacker, it can't be these kids, man. I just don't want to believe that teenagers carry knives and go around stabbing people in alleyways. I want to speak to them myself!'

'That policeman is going to find them - he'll ask', assured Knacker, pouring himself more tea.

'You don't get the truth when you're a copper, you get the version of the truth that someone hopes makes them look their best. It's like online dating!'

'Never done that.'

'Well, you don't put your profile as 'pushing forty, very large but cock not in proportion, halitosis and athlete's foot', right.'

'Right, I know where you're coming from, but I'm worried it turns into *something* worse - pack mentality or whatever!'

'That happens but it's often fuelled by alcohol isn't it, lowered inhibitions, more susceptible to persuasion and all that. I'll text the lads and say no drink, *all* business.'

'They'll *love* that!'

'We can still sit and have craic - don't *need* drink for that!'

'Fair enough.'

'We will just be keeping an eye out for *them* while we're doing it.'

'Yeah. okay. What time was it?'

'*Six*, you useless prick!'

'I know, I know!'

'Anyhoo, that's not why we're here is it; I *really* need your advice dude. Hughesy should be here as well by now.'

'You're worried about being a parent?'

'Worried...*absolutely* bricking it mate!'

'Honestly, there's nothing I can say that will make you feel *any* better!'

'Thanks a fucking bunch!'

'I mean, I can tell you everything you wanna know, and give you all the advice in the world, but it's a life that you made by slinging a baby in her or whatever you called it, and so you will remain terrified!'

'Lads, lads, dads!'

'This one wants reassurance about being a parent, Hughesy!'

'No chance', replied Hughesy, sitting down. 'There's literally nothing at all I can tell you that will make you feel at ease with impending parenthood.'

'Told ya!'

'Right, well I asked you two to meet up to hopefully give me advice, to put my mind at ease, you know?'

'Can't do it. See you later!' Hughesy and Knacker both stood to leave.

'Very funny. There's books and groups and midwives and *everything* for Sarah, but I'm at a complete loss!'

'What's the main worry?'

'I don't know...probably that I'll be a rubbish Dad?'

'You will be! Every first time Dad is awful mate, because they don't have boobs!'

'You do!'

'Piss off - I mean we can *try* to do the right thing, to look after the baby, to look after the lady, to make sure everyone is fine and organise the visitors and the treats and that, but no matter what, the woman is designed to be maternal and when everything else will fail to appease an upset kid, she can say 'give her here' and all is well.'

'Yeah, we have to try to do what we can but we are pretty redundant - until the kid eats real food and reacts to silly faces, a Dad is essentially a babysitter having an absolute meltdown at *all* times.'

'Well, this is worse than I thought!'

'No, it isn't, because you now know that every other father ever in the history of all babymaking has felt like that, you can feel like a complete abject failure safe in the knowledge that so did they.'

'So basically, I'm wishing away the first half a year?'

'Kind of not - it's still awesome even though you'll be shit at it. The smiles, the cuddles and that. After that though, you're just trying to keep them alive until they move out at as young an age as possible! If you can marry them off at sixteen, do it, otherwise they'll be sponging away all your money forever!'

'Right.'

'You'll be fine mate, just don't forget the push present like I did.'

'What's a push present?'

'The woman gets a keepsake type of gift after giving birth, mate.'

'Does she?'

'Yeah but think on before buying it - and don't present the present the second the kid is out!'

'Think on?'

'Well, don't buy something like an anklet when her feet will be four times the size!'

'Why would her *feet* be bigger?'

'Nobody knows, not even science, but feet and ankles swell up like a blebbed football in the last month of pregnancy!'

'And their tits get *really* itchy!'

'What?'

'Not even kidding. One of the reasons it's so exhausting when the bairn arrives is because you've been battling back the demons inside your missus for months.'

'What else - I'm going to make a list to look out for! Then I can maybe help and she'll feel better.'

'That's nice mate, but be warned that nothing you ever *say* or *do* will ever be right again! From the start of the second trimester her emotions will bounce between rage and tears at least four times an hour.'

'And it's understandable as well, because she's going to be having headaches, nausea, heartburn…'

'Aye, our lass was drinking Gaviscon the same way she drank Apple Sourz when we met!'

'…she'll be really tired at the end because obviously she's carrying a human leeching all the good out of her body, but I bet she's been tired at the start as well yeah?'

'Yeah, what's that all about?'

'The emotional turmoil of bringing another *you* into the world!'

'Fair.'

'I'm not done!'

'What?'

'She's going to have dry skin on her feet or her elbows or *somewhere* random, and get spots on her face which just adds to the angertears, and her favourite food one day will be turned down the next like you've just offered her a plate of your own shit!'

'Fu...wow!'

'Good luck abstaining from the swearing through the next eighteen years dude!'

'Oh, and to add to everything he's said, she'll turn into a superhero who can smell any smell a hundred feet away, and no matter what it smells like, it's *bad*! She'll walk in the front door and her eye will start twitching and she'll be screaming 'what's that smell?' Next thing she's scurrying 'round the floor sniffing at the skirting boards absolutely enraged at you that you can't smell a thing with your non-preggers, human nose.'

'So, you excited?'

'Oh yeah, much better now lads, thanks a million! The hot bird I fell for is going to turn into all the Avengers - anger of Hulk, senses of Spider-Man, beard of Iron-Man, but most definitely *not* the arse of Black Widow!'

'I've got a load of stuff in the loft at home - I'll dig it all out and pass it on, just monitors, thermometers, a sleepyhead pillow thing and that!'

'Cheers, man. What about the thighmaster?'

'Thighmaster? Fucking hell Jane Fonda, what do you want one of *them* for?'

'For Sarah, isn't it?'

'She will definitely not appreciate a thighmaster with a vag like Freddie Krueger's fingerpuppet!'

'You said something about your lass having her second thighmaster!'

'Trimester! It's a third of the pregnancy - you've got a *lot* of reading to do.'

'Yeah, I think I have.'
'How are you feeling about the wedding?'
'Don't even get me started on that; we've just had the bloody engagement party and she wants us married *before* the baby comes!'
'You're not getting married just because you're almost over the hill and there's a baby on the way are you?'
'No, I'm genuinely not. It's love lads, I just hadn't realised it until she was out of my life. I proposed on the beach, before I knew about the baby!'
'Ah, mint!'
'Nice one. We were all a bit worried you were being trafficked as a husband and baby daddy.'
'Ha, no! Should we get the bill - it's on me?'
'Had I known that I would have had some of those cakes!'
'Yeah, excuse me...bill please.'
'Right, so Friday at six, VG, remind the others and tell them it's strictly no alcohol!'
'Sure. You walking home?'
'Going to put a bet on, then I've got to call into work.'
'Okay, bye mate!'
'Hey, we didn't even talk about the actual baby!'
'Oh, that's for another day!'
'I don't know if I want to know.'
'It's not *all* bad.'
'*Mostly*, but not all!'
'Spot on, see you then.'
'Later, dads!'

-

'Here you are, Sir.'
'Thank you, keep the change.'
'Thanks...can I just say something, if *you* don't mind? I know it's rude but I couldn't help overhearing your friends and despite what they've said, trust me, your partner is going through the worst bit! You can be worried and scared and lost, but at least you'll be doing it with your penis intact! If you go home saying what they've said to you, it probably won't be!'
'Great...cheers.'

'No problem, Sir! Come again!'
'Doubt I ever will after what I've heard today!

-

At the end of the street, as Cookie left the coffee shop, Hughesy was waiting in line.

'I've recently come into a *lot* of money, you see, so what's the harm in betting it away? Besides, I've got a fella on the inside tells me this pony is going to jog home!'

'Okay, Sir, just checking - it is a larger bet than we're used to *you* placing, that's all.'

'Aye, well, when you've got luck on your side you may as well keep riding it!'

'There you go, Sir. That's been placed.'

'Thank you, I'll be back tomorrow for me winnings! Mark me words!'

As the elderly gentleman turned to leave, Hughesy recognised him immediately and left his place in the queue to catch up to him by the door.

'Wait!'

'What do you want?'

'I'm Hughesy, Gaz's mate - do you remember me?'

'Hughesy, Hughesy - yes, I do. *Gary* is dead. Fuck off.'

'I know, and I want to know why you're acting like it's the best thing that *ever* happened to you!'

'What do you mean?'

'Throwing money around, what is it…'

'Life insurance!'

'…thought as much! You have *always* been a vile excuse for a father, but this just proves it.'

'Get out of my way, you've got *no* idea…'

'I know *everything* you did! That speech at the crematorium doesn't make you a better person - how did you not even realise he'd not been home?'

'So you were one of *them* causing bother at the crem as well, eh? Leave me alone.'

'Are you okay there, Sirs?'

'Yeah, we're fine', replied Hughesy, as Gaz's dad took the opportunity to leave the shop, disappearing into thin air before Hughesy could see where he went. Standing looking both ways, dumbfounded, Cookie drove past and raised a hand. Hughesy nodded and went back inside.

Interlude:

Shattering across the floor, the photograph of them fishing together - which seemed eternities ago now - flew from the wall as the door struggled to hold back the force slamming against it.

'I'm sorry, I'm sorry! *Please…*'

'Open this fucking door you little shit…mark me words…'

'No, I'm sorry! Calm down, please…'

'Calm down? Calm fu...*right!*'

Silence spilled into the room. Crushed against the farthest wall, between the foot of the bed and the wardrobe, a second to breathe settled.

'Oh, than…'

The door fell forwards, crashing onto the rug and rattling the toys and keepsakes on the shelves. Propelled by momentum and rage, the beast lay on top of it in the centre of the room. Then, it was onto all fours, then knees, then stood.

Then moving.

'Dad, I'm *sorry!*'

'Get out of there, you little *fucking* coward! Letting people hit *you*? I'll fucking teach you!'

He started stamping his work boot into the gap between the wardrobe and bed, connecting repeatedly with his left shin. To make it stop, he pushed himself forward into the room, but couldn't stand. His father kicked him in the gut, again and again, until he wasn't crying out loud anymore. His face was contorted into an agonising yawn of pain, but he could no longer make a sound, such was the fire in his leg and the ice in his stomach.

'Now, *get up*, you worthless little sack of shit!'

He was dragged to his feet, down the stairs, and a couple of streets across the estate past the shop - people looked at him in disgust while saying hello to his dad - and to the house of the boy who had hit him.

He watched as his Dad knocked, waited, and then dragged the man from his doorway. On the grass, he stamped and kicked, slashing with his hands and screaming venom, until the man was a ball. The neighbours looked over at the noise, but none moved. Content that he had inflicted pain and enough people had seen or heard, he dragged the man by his neck over to the step in front of the door, laid his head next to it, said something to the boy and then stepped back and kicked as hard as he could, slamming his boot into one side and crushing the other side against the solid stone.

    Both seven year old boys screamed.

    As he was dragged home, people kept nodding their greetings to his father.

Chapter 10: Friday, 18:00

'*Everyone* here? On time? That doesn't compute!'
'I know, even Knacker - fully clothed thank fuck!'
As Lee and Bucky walked up through the canopy of trees by the school, and around the right hand edge of the boating lake toward the small metal bridge, the others came into view. The maniacally smiling cartoon face stared helplessly out of the 'O' in Happy Shopper still, but everything else about the VG was exactly the same as it had been in their youth, and that you had been transported back in time was a feeling which did not fade each time they saw the place. Lying half on his side, with one leg bent up and one elbow propping his body from the grass itself, Cookie was the first they spotted, then Knacker - but only because he was on the other side of the slight hill. The rest were either already sat down or were walking toward the group from the direction of the VG.

'Lads, good to see you all once again for the very first time.'
'No alcohol?'
'None, I swear - not a drop, no sirree, not from me, bevvy free, total tee!'
'What's up with you, then?'
'He reckons he has a *plan*.'
'Bucky man, no plan! *Okay*. We're going to get some answers if we spot these shitballs but other than that there's no pranks, no silliness, no accidents and definitely no fucking drinking!'
'Who died and put you in charge?'
'Unfortunately, *most* people.'
'Haha brutal!'
'I was just relieved to get here and see all of you - started worrying one of us dies every time we try a get-together like we're being picked off in a horror movie or something!'
'Not quite *that* bad.'
'Not far enough wrong though!'
'Lads', said kev, returning with Dave from the VG, 'we've just seen the bloke from Gaz's funeral in there, in the shop.'

'What bloke?'

'Young skinny one, he was sat opposite side to that copper!'

'Oh yeah, I didn't even see him leave the crem!'

'Me neither, must have left *after* we'd gone to the pub.'

'Who was he then? Didn't know Gaz had a cousin or *anything*, growing up?'

'Dunno, he scarpered!'

'What do you mean?'

'Well, he was in front of us in the queue, and I said 'nice watch' - it was the classic Casio type, like Gaz had on for the retro effect - and he turns around, looks at us like Kevin before he steals the toothbrush, then he's off like a dart.'

'Who the hell is Kevin?'

'Home Alone, when he's in the shop and the old bloke comes along next to him and for some bizarre reason never explained slams his bandaged hand down on the counter and stares intimidatingly at a small child.'

'You've thought too much about that!'

'But I now know exactly what you mean about the lad's reaction!'

'Well, where did he go? We've not noticed anyone come around this way or down the path!'

'No sign...must have ran off into the houses next to the VG.'

'Weird.'

'Is it? He was at a relative's funeral, or a colleagues, and then we turned up and made the vicar shout the c-word - I'd run away from us as well.'

'Cornflour?'

'Cabbages?'

'Cribbage?'

'Is it a vicar? I've heard people say pastor, priest, all sorts...what's right?'

'I dunno. Defo not *'penguin'* though - he didn't like *that*!'

'Why did he have Gaz's watch?'

'He didn't, that policeman said at Cookie's party that his watch, wallet and everything were found at his house.'

'His *Dad's* house! I wanted to tell you all this face-to-face lads, rather than in a message...I bumped into Gaz's Da at the bookies, and he was *bragging* about the money he'd come into!'

'What, from Gaz's death?'

'Yep! He even admitted it was the life insurance, no fucking shame!'

'What a twisted, horrible old bastard - never changed, I fucking *told you* at the crem! Didn't I?'

'Yeah mate, you're right. Wouldn't have been him who attacked Gaz though.'

'Maybe he set it up?'

'This isn't a novel or a film mate - it's real life. People don't really arrange the murders of their family!'

'Oh pal, I'm taking it you haven't got Netflix!'

'What do *we* do now, then? Go looking for this lad? He may know of someone who had it in for Gaz if he was a mate or a relative or something!'

'Hey, hey, the gang's *all* here!'

They all turned, to see a familiar face approaching them across the crest of the hill behind.

'Hedz?'

'Alright mate...what are *you* doing *here*?'

'Aye-aye lads - Bucky invited me, sorry I'm late! You all look *deep* in conversation, what's up?'

'It's a long story!'

'What the fuck, Bucky?', whispered Lee, 'you didn't tell me about this; what have you invited this *junky* for?'

'I can hear you, by the way.'

'Sorry, Hedz, but I don't want to hang about with someone who hasn't changed since school, and is still scraping by off his face!'

'I think I may have some explaining to do, lads, if you will give me a minute?'

'*One* minute!', added Cookie, 'if I'd seen you at my party I would have thrown you down the stairs!'

'Okay...so first things first I am absolutely one hundred percent *not* a junky, but I do sell drugs. *All* the drugs.'

'Fuck's sakes, man!'

'Hey, I've got a minute! I sold drugs at school and you all bought them so don't be so judgey! Then I went to college, and then uni, then had a pretty decent job and never made money as easily as I did at school. As a young'un I didn't have ethics, but as an adult I gained scruples and for a couple of years in my mid-twenties I thought about building a business…'

'A *business*?'

'…thirty seconds left, you! So *finally* I changed careers, and set up a much more ethically sound version of the business I ran at school. All sales are made through a website, and all buyers are vetted and age checked. I limit amounts that customers may buy in a certain time period and deliver personally, so there aren't little versions of me running around at an impressionable school age. I am *definitely* not scraping by and I am *not* on drugs - haven't touched them since we were at college and I nearly got caught smoking a joint and kicked out.'

'That doesn't explain your behaviour at the party!'

'Yeah, that was not good. So, I went to drop something off, a regular customer, and he says to meet him at the big club, function room toilets! I'm just handing over a handful of E when this bloody off-duty bobby walks in, I didn't even think I just threw them in me mouth so he didn't see them.'

'Oh we know him, kind of!'

'Aw mate, this sounds too ridiculous to not be true!'

'I'm serious, I vaguely recollected seeing you lot, then Bucky messaged me on Facebook and clarified it. Sorry for the way I went on, *whatever* it was I did!'

'You thought you were in the *past* mate!'

'In the words of the great philosopher, Ice Cube, 'You don't get high on your own supply!'

'I was in a bad way the next day - been so long since I'd been clean - and the wife's going off it that I've scrawled 'Great Scot!' across the living room walls in the kids' finger paints!'

'Wife and kids?'

'Yeah...don't demonise people based on their chosen profession! I'm running a successful business, an *essential* public service! I'm just like you!'

'Okay, okay...sorry for what I said. I thought you were here because of drugs!', said Lee.

Hedz and Bucky exchanged a glance, before the latter cleared his throat and rose to his feet, one arm a mauve hue and almost back to normal size.

'I don't like *this*', said Knacker.

'A tribute, lads, is only truly a tribute if it in some way represents the person you are paying tribute *to*!'

'Did he keep notes?'

'Gaz liked to drink awful vinegary-tasting piss - that's off the menu. Gaz liked to spend time with the boys - check. Gaz loved - LOVED - getting high!'

'Oh no...'

'So, with immediate effect...'

'We're all in the past!'

'...I declare the Gaz Tribute Smoke-out Session officially begun!'

'Shit! Shit! *Shit*!'

'We are definitely too old for *this*...'

'Did we give Foz the send-off he deserved?'

'Well, no it was an absolute shitshow!'

'Total balls-up, Bucky mate!'

'Did we end up scattering his ashes up at the Cem, over the lights of the town below? A place *he* loved?'

'Purely by coincidence and Hughesy's kleptomania!'

'Okay, there's obviously no point fighting this.'

'Good! So, there are a number of rules for the Gaz Tribute Smoke-out Session, that should be followed at *all* times. Rule number one - we are all older and unhealthier so we pick one drug each and that's it. We aren't mixing them all over the place! B - you have to give the rest of us a head's up the second you think you're going to whitey! We don't need PC Plod turning up again. Finally, four - you *don't* get off your face, we are still here mainly to try and find out what happened to Gaz.'

'And we haven't got a wheelbarrow to carry you!'

'It's a slight relief that there's not a wheelbarrow full of paraphernalia, if I'm honest.'

'Well, actually, we don't need a wheelbarrow, lads!', added Hedz.

Chapter 11: Friday, 19:00

'Opening his jacket like the wings of a demented bat, Hedz began 'Bucky said it would be a tame affair, so I've not brought *any* of the opioids…'

'Opioids?'

'The china white mate, brown horse...heroin!'

'So if there's no heroin it's a *quiet* night? Fuck me!'

'I probably would if there was heroin!'

'But I have brought your standard *stimulants*: cocaine, meth - *club drugs* like MDMA, ket - *hallucinogens*: marijuana, LSD - and alcohol is a *depressant* but you're staying off it, so I brought some benzo in its place!'

'Fucking hell, Hedz - I thought you'd just bring some dope!', exclaimed Bucky.

'Naw mate, bad shit that!'

'Dope's not even addictive is it?'

'Massively impacts people's wellbeing dope does lads, mainly because it's 'not dangerous' so people just allow it to be part of their everyday life while it makes them paranoid and susceptible to mental breaks.'

'That true?'

'Yeah, I've read about that as well.'

'Right, I'll have LSD then mate!'

'Wait a minute Dave...what the smeg are we doing? Are you *serious*?'

'It's absolutely ridiculous, and stupid, and I'm going to regret it, and yes we are too old for this shit, but it is what Gaz would have wanted?'

'Really? Just 'cos he was a stoner doesn't mean he would want you to kill yourself having a heart attack on acid!'

'Giz it here, Hedz.'

'I'll have a joint, mate!' said Lee.

'Yeah, is everyone else just having a bit green?'

'I'm abstaining lads', said Cookie. 'I do *actually* see some sort of logic to the tribute, I can't even believe I'm saying that, but I'm really trying to control my emotions and that's a struggle without foreign substances in my system. You get that?'

'Yeah, no worries mate.'

'Tell you what, if someone has to get cracked on the skull by an OAP I will do that in loving memory instead, yeah?'

'Deal!'

'Sure about *this*?', Hughesy asked Dave. 'Just have a joint with the rest of us!'

'I'm fine - look I literally live just over there, I'm with you lot, and I fucking *hated* weed back in the day! That weird taste in your mouth like flat cola and nettles, the fuzzy, foggy head, I only did it because everyone else did it! I always took the shortest draw and passed it on the quickest.'

'Just say no, then.'

'Can't do that!'

'Why? We're adults mate, there's no peer pressure anymore, there's no need to show off when you don't need to.'

'It's not that, I want to say goodbye to Gaz and as messed up as it is, Bucky's *right*!'

'Like the twilight zone whenever anyone says that!'

'*And* I'm nearly forty; I love my life with Michael but I don't try new things - everything is *safe*...I think I know what I mean...'

'I get you. I've got you! I'll stick next to you though!'

While Dave and Hughesy talked, Hedz had sat and rolled seven joints. The others, except Cookie whose eyes never left the shop in front of him, watched in nostalgic awe. As he had done when they were kids, Hedz seemed to have four hands moving independently of each other while he connected the Rizlas, sprinkled in the baccy, crumbled on the resin, used the ripped up pieces of Rizla packet to form a roach for each joint, and twisted them closed. In the time that Hughesy had spent checking on Dave, all ingredients had appeared, been used, and were gone again, leaving just the uniform white soldiers lined up on the grass between them all.

'Okay, now take it *easy*, for some of you it's been over twenty years, and things may have changed *slightly* as well.'

'Just a joint, mate!'

'We smoked that many of these back in the day one little one isn't going to do much is it!', laughed Kev.

'Cheers for being sensible, Hedz, but we're all good.'

'Lighter anyone?'

Hedz produced a lighter with each hand from somewhere in his jacket, passing one to each side which made their way around the circle and both ended up at Cookie.

Chapter 12: Friday, 19:30

'All I'm saying lads is that Gaz is *not* an angel now!', drawled Lee.

'*What* is he then?'

'Gaz dead, baby...Gaz dead.'

'No, he's not *just* dead!'

'Is he a fairy?'

'Like Dave?'

'Or a dragon?'

'Whose motorcycle is this?'

'I mean when you die there's not anything *else* - the way you live on is through everyone you touched!'

'Cookie will live *forever*!'

'Hmmm, at least I touch consenting adults', acknowledged Cookie, not really listening to their meandering conversation.

'So what about religion and God?'

'Who created *God*? Godgod?'

'I believe in all that!'

'Really?'

'Yeah - it's helped me through some tough times.'

'So has Pornhub!'

'I thought that's what we were talking about?'

'No, religion!'

'Ah, the crazies?'

'Whose chopper is this?'

'Not crazies, I mean I get *why* people believe in something, but you see people trying to do right for some sort of reward after death or something - '

'People should all just do right because it's *right*, you mean?'

'Yeah. There's no justice, or karma, or any of that bullocks...bollshit...crap!'

'If there was then Foz and Gaz would be *here*.'

'Who created *Godgod* though? Godgodgod?'

'Very different things that happened to them - Gaz had no say in *his* end!'

'We can't even talk about Gaz yet because we don't know *why* it happened, or *how* it happened!', said Cookie.

'Do you think Foz had a *say*?'

'Yeah! He chose it!'

'Naw, I think he did what he did because he had *no* choice!'

'Of course he fucking did! That's why I've been so angry at him!', seethed Mitch.

'*Angry*?'

'Where is Dave?'

'Me too', added Hughesy.

'Kev as well', said Kev.

'I just feel so *sad* all the time. That he felt he couldn't go on. How can *you* feel anger?'

'Kev feels angry that Foz left Kev, and that Foz didn't know *we* were here for him, and that Kev didn't realise there was something wrong, and that Kev *couldn't* help, and never can, and that Foz abandoned us.'

'I thought you *were* Kev?'

'Kev *is* Kev!', mumbled Kev.

'I felt guilty for feeling angry lads...I didn't know anyone else did!'

'I've just felt so sad all the time, I didn't think of anger, but now you say it I'm angry at us!'

'Who created *Godgodgod* though? Was it Godgodgodgod?'

'One of you wasters punch Bucky square in the mouth please', stated Cookie, not turning toward them.

'I *still* can't get my head around Foz...'

'Dingdingdingding we have a winner!'

'Say what you see!'

'...shut it Roy! And I feel like I should be grieving *more* for Gaz but I'm not ready to move on yet. I don't have the grief stockpiled to just dish out to more than one at a time. That makes *me* feel guilty.'

'Gents', said Hedz, 'if I may interrupt - all of these feelings are *completely* normal, you know!'

'I feel like my arms have been unscrewed and my feet are floating away...'

'Well, maybe not all. Look, I don't know if you remember my brother, Chris, he was a few years below us at school - *we* lost *him* to suicide when he was 18.'

'Hedz, man -'

'It's something I've lived with for nearly twenty years and it *does not* get easier, but every single emotion you feel *is* the right one. Don't second guess or feel guilty for being angry or too sad, and guilt *is* the big one. You will always spend time thinking what if, what if, *what if* but there's no second chances at life...whether you believe in afterlife or not, God or not, it *doesn't* matter! You can't do anything now that they're gone and because of that, you won't ever be able to stop thinking you could have done something when they were here. You won't.'

'I didn't know that, dude.'

'It was years after you'd all moved on, I was even at Uni so I wasn't *here*. It wasn't depression or anything, which I think it was for Foz from what they said at his funeral…'

'You were *there*?'

'Yeah, nice arse Kev!'

'Kev *is* sorry!'

'…with Chris it was drugs. He was high and he just did it. No note, no calls for help, too much in his system to fight against it once his self-protection would have kicked in, and next thing you know there's one more chair in the kitchen that you don't need!'

'Fuck, man!'

'I knew your Chris. I was in his year at school.'

Hedz turned and saw the officer standing behind him. Cookie looked over briefly, said 'creepy bas...bugger' and turned back to the shop. The policeman had walked over the grass, completely in the open, directly behind Hedz, with only Cookie looking the other way. The others had been so concentrated on their own guilt, anger, sadness and floating feet that they had not seen him at all until he spoke.

Chapter 13: Friday: 19:45

'That's them there!'
'*You* had a fight with that lot?'
'Yeah, kind of.'
'Why do you think they're back?'
'I don't know.'
'Why do you think they've got the police with them?'
'I don't know!'

-

'Were you?', asked Hedz, as he slowly buttoned up his jacket.
'Yeah...we were good mates, actually. I was often at your house growing up.'
'I don't remember *you*.'
'That's the big brother effect isn't it? I couldn't pick my little brother's friends out of a line-up now, but I bet they all remembered looking up to me.'
'You looked up to *me*?'
'Of course, the older brother is always the cool one. You were Chris's hero, too! Everything always came back to you! Did you know he once told our Maths teacher you would come back from college and knack him if he kept us at lunch?'
'No way.'
'Yeah...guy kept us at lunch for the rest of the week after that!'
'Haha Chrissy man!'
'You couldn't have done *anything*, by the way. And I know you're all feeling it about Forrester but I blamed *myself* for not being there when Chris had bought the stuff, or when he'd gone up into the woods, but we can't do that - you *cannot* be responsible for the actions you *never* took in places you *never* were. When it's a sudden, reactionary event, rather than a build-up of emotions or traumas, feeling guilty would be like regretting not being there to pull someone back who got hit by a car...it's a random, tragic event!'

'But with Foz', said Mitch, 'for us, it *was* building up. There could have been *something* we did, if we'd thought to message, or call!'

'But we saw a social media smile and didn't look beyond that - '

'*Where's* Dave?'

'Look, I don't have answers, I just spent *years* beating myself up over Chris and even became a copper to try and make a difference to kids...and drugs...'

'Yeah, same!'

'*You're* police?'

'No, *no*', hastened Hedz.

'Anyway, that's not why I was coming over. Two things: first off, you can smell you lot from the shop!'

'Lee, which pants are you wearing?'

The sombre mood lifted as they all started giggling. Even Cookie cracked a smile.

'Second, the last thing you all said at the party the other week...congratulations, by the way...was that you wouldn't do anything *stupid*.'

'We *are* stupid!'

'Great defence, Bucky!'

'So why are you all here? And why are *you* staring at the shop like you're going to rip it out of the ground?'

'We're just having a proper send-off.'

'He just hates shops! Still salty they closed Rumbelows!'

They all giggled again.

'Here, I've got a question for you, completely not related to anything at all to do with why *we're* here, but who was the *other bloke* at Gaz's funeral?'

'His dad?'

'No there was another, sat on the other side to you!'

'Oh, he crept in, didn't notice him until you lot caused a scene. He was up and out straight after as well. Looked young, slim build, brown hair. Couldn't tell you anything else about him, I'm afraid.'

'We think it may be a relative.'

'Mr. Parlour mentioned there were no siblings *or* cousins at one point, I'm sure.'

Right, cheers.'

'I've got a question as well; have you spoken to those kids yet?'

'We're making enquiries, following up on some discussions, that's why I pulled up and spotted you lot, actually. Despite everything you're going through, stay *out of it*, *don't* get in trouble, *don't* hang around here, and *don't* smoke marijuana in a public place - what impression are you giving any teenagers that walk past?'

'Yeah, okay, okay - it was a tribute that's all.'

'Well it easily leads onto heavier stuff! I'll be around here a while, I want you lot gone.'

'Where *is* Dave?'

'I think he took my feet.'

Chapter 14: Friday, 20:00

'I've text Michael, Dave's not at home, Michael's coming.'
'Are you sure he's not at home then? *Eh*?'
'I need food.'
'Same. What food?'
'All.'
'Town then? Ten minute walk.'
'I feel like I'm walking in porridge!'
'Twenty minute walk if you've got porridgefeet then!'

The group started walking across the small metal bridge separating the long shallow pool of water from the larger boating lake, as Michael came running down the path. They heard him first, not because he shouted or because of the sound of his sprinting footsteps, but rather because of the squeaking noise.

'Mick!'
'Michael', gasped Michael.
'What are *you* doing *here*, Mickey lad?'
'I literally just told you all I'd text him and he was on his way!'
'Oh yeah.'
'Mike, have you seen my feet?'
'What...what about them?', asked Michael, looking down.
'I can't find them!'
'What the hell have you all been doing?'
'Not all', said Cookie. 'Why've you brought *that* thing?'
'David was supposed to return it to Bucky anyway, and then I remembered Gaz spent the night in it and thought you would want it here, but *now* I'm thinking we may need it to carry you lot!'
'Mikey, I am so high!'
'That's wonderful - where did you old men get drugs from?'
'Hi, I'm Hedz!'
'We've met before, in a toilet!'
'I think you've got me confused with…'
'At Cookie's party! You tried to sell me drugs.'

'...ah *right*. That was not a fair representation of me at all. I've explained to the gents what happened. Sorry about that!'

Michael looked to Cookie, who nodded. 'Where's Dave then?', he asked, as they rounded the right perimeter of the lake and began to enter the canopy of trees next to the school fence.

'Michael!!!'

They all looked up.

'Michael michael hello help I flew like a bird I'm a bird a big bird look at these wings look at my beak I'm so much birdy tweet tweet nest where's my nest oh no oh no bird got no nest all my pretty chickens - '

'Dave mate haha!'

'David, this is *not* funny. What on earth are you doing? Get *down*!'

'It's a *bit* funny.'

'Not get down fly soar whoosh flap flap beautiful bird magnificent bird...'

'He hasn't had a joint! What's he had?'

'He had an acid tab, mate. I promised *I'd* look after him but Hedz was telling a sad story and I was crying.'

'Acid? David, we are trying to adopt and if you get arrested then we cannot, can we!'

'Pretty chickens?'

'Get down *now*!'

With that, Dave spread his wings, squawked twice and flew from the tree.

Chapter 15: Friday, 20:15

Some shop fronts had changed, there wasn't a Rumbelows anymore, but mostly the town centre was as it had been when they were kids. The ten of them entered through a covered archway next to the leisure centre, before spilling out into the wider main paved area. Rectangular in shape, but slightly narrower at the far end, the town consisted of two rows of shops facing inwards towards each other. The council had put trees in the middle, randomly spaced with seats around them, to look prettier; they served more as a stark reminder that concrete was winning over nature. After the events on the way to town, they were all pretty much sober of mind and hungry of belly instead.

'There was a kebab shop 'round the back of town back in the day!'

'Yeah, that's *still* there actually', said Hedz, who was still being eyed with disgust by Michael.

'Brill, there then?'

'Or Dominoes?'

'There's a Dominoes?'

'Yeah, next to Tesco!'

'There's a *Tesco*?'

'There have been *some* changes over the last twenty years you know.'

'Actually, it's more like add-ons than changes', added Michael. 'Dave always says this town is like a Lego set completed in the seventies, that some daft kid stuck a bit of Meccano to in the twenty-first century!'

'What's that even *mean*?'

'Town has had some things done to it over time that have not made any difference, and just look out of place!'

'Oh, like glitter on a dog shit!'

'Yes, *that* popular old saying!'

'Whatever happened to *white* dogshit?'

'Why would you wonder that?'

'Whatever happened to two dogs getting stuck together?'

'That happened all the time, didn't it!'

'They must have evolved.'

'How's *he* doing?'
'He's alright, you know. Just keeps dozing off.'
'Are you sure we don't need an ambulance?'
'Not until he's completely lucid!'
'Is that right, *you're* going to adopt?'
'We've started looking into it. I can't *believe* he's done this though. Peer pressure!'
'Woah, we actively tried to get him to have a joint instead!'
'Oh well what fine upstanding pillars you are, I do apologise.'
'Pillocks of the community, us!'
'What's on *your* mind, Cookie?', asked Lee.
'We need to go back to the VG soon as.'
'Why?'
'While that copper was rabbitting on one of those little twats was looking around the side of the shop!'
'Piss off, let's go *straight* back then?'
'You heard what he said, he's gonna be there a while. We'll get you lot fed and head back.'
'Just be careful if you do catch up with them - we don't know if they were involved but you can be sure they'll have an attitude - don't want you losing your rag!'
'Who's on the rag? You Lee? Good job you've worn dark pants!'
'Cheers, Lee, but I'm fine. Kid on the way, I'm in control.'
'They do speed awareness courses on Zoom!'
'You what, Kev?'
'They do! Fucking brilliant!'
'Why's that brilliant?'
'It's on *Zoom*!'
'Wish he was still searching for his feet.'
'Hey, Stephens has gone! I loved it in there; when I was little I would stand in front of that *massive* sweet counter and drool!'
'You still drool!'
'First ever job was there - paper round when I was thirteen!', said Bucky.
'I remember that - you'd come straight to mine for school but it was always like seven o'clock still!'

'I'd sit with your Da and watch Big Breakfast and eat all your cereal while you got ready! Good times!'

'Not for me being left with the own brand soggy cardboard cornflakes!'

'I miss your Da!'

'Why?'

'He was a good bloke!'

'He *still* fucking *is* you retard!'

'Is he alive?'

'I bloody hope so!'

'Mustn't have been on a sober night out with you lot then!'

'Okay mickey boy…'

'Michael!'

'…*we're* sorry, *we're* morons, *we're* completely responsible for the actions of *your* grown-up husband babydaddy!'

'Or babymammy...how does it work?'

'Okay, it was his choice to take it, I'm just annoyed, and I have no idea. We haven't discussed roles.'

'I just meant names.'

'We're not going to call one of us *'mammy'*.'

'That'll be confusing!'

'It's the twentytwenties, Mitch! Our child will be *loved*, not confused!'

'I meant for you two...when it shouts 'Dad' and you *both* come running!'

'That is *actually* a good point!'

'Remember the ramp that used to go up there', said Hughesy, pointing at the place where the town narrowed. 'On market day we'd stand at the top and shout…'

'Maaaaaaaaam…'

'Maaaaaaaam…'

'Maaaaaaaam…'

They all shouted in unison.

'And *every* woman in the town would look up! Absolute lame classic!'

'Boyes, boys! Where the infamous flask of De'ath was purchased', nodded Mitch toward a mobile phone shop in the corner.

They reached the end of the main street of shops, and turned left onto a shorter, narrower area.

'Boozebusters was there, and Blockbusters next door!'

'I remember that!'

'Would get sent in Blocks to choose three films for the week while me Ma went in Boozes.'

'Remember that, getting your films *out*, bloody hell.'

'Remember that bloke with the eyes so wonky if he cried it would run down his back, worked in the video shop? When you returned them he would open each one and put it in the recorder behind the desk to check it was totally rewound! You could fucking see through the little windows!'

'Oh aye, he did that to us as well! My Dad once asked him if his eye was trying to rewind around his head. Thought it was hilarious back in the day, but it doesn't sound as good now.'

'We're conditioned by political correctness, that's why!'

'No, I think I'm just old enough to know right from wrong.'

They turned left again, and saw the welcome lights of the Kebab shop. Dave began to shift in his makeshift seat.

'I really hate it when people say 'but', you know.'

'*But* why?'

'Not like *that*, I mean 'I'm not sexist but…' really irritates me.'

'There always is a but, though, a legitimate one!'

'Naw, if you say 'I'm not racist but…' then you're going to say something racist!'

'Not at all true.'

'Example?'

'I'm not racist but...black people are better at basketball!'

'That's true, but it's not racist at all, it's a compliment!'

'Racism isn't negative, it's *both*. It's just saying something about a lot of people based on one thing, skin colour! Just like any stereotype there's good and bad.'

'I've got one…I'm not sexist but...when a woman appears on Soccer Saturday I never trust her as much as the men.'

'*That's* sexist mate!'

'Proper Richard Keys there sunshine!'

'How about', suggested Michael, 'I'm not homophobic but...gay men have a better skincare regime!'

'Ooh me, I'm not ageist but...that twenty-year-old *cannot* be a lollipop lady!'

'That's good! Why *is* that the case?'

'At some point in history it was decided that the best people to save children from being crushed by motorcars would be the old, frail and slow!'

'How did you know Foz knew?'

'Dave's awake!'

'What do you mean?'

'I asked you this before and didn't get an answer, at the park; you all knew that Foz knew I was gay?'

'So he messaged us all once, back in the MySpace days it was, and asked who else was coming to your wedding!'

'Ah...'

'We all replied 'what wedding' and he said, basically, 'oops'. He apologised, thought it best that it come from you.'

'Which it *never* did!'

'Sorry, lads. I was a fool.'

'*Was?*'

'Michael what the fuck are *you* doing here? I can explain, I felt faint...'

'I was here before you were in the wheelbarrow.'

'Where was I?'

'In a tree. Quoting Shakespeare. Trying to *fly*!'

'Shit. We need to talk then, yeah?'

'Oh yes.'

Chapter 16: Friday, 20:30

'It was a few weeks ago, and CCTV from the shop shows who was involved in the altercation outside!'

'Right then, yeah I *was* there!'

'Do you want to clarify what happened?'

'My brother and his mates made me ask people to go in the shop for us, you know!'

'For alcohol?'

'Yeah...and I asked this one bloke who was just a *proper* dickhead, told me to, you know, like, bang my mam!'

'Then what?'

'I went up home, we live through there, behind the shop don't we! I told *them* what had been said and they dragged me back down here!'

'What, did they come to the shop specifically to find this man?'

'Yeah!'

'With the *intention* of being violent?'

'Well, yeah I guess!'

'Did any of them bring a weapon?'

'No, we wouldn't ever do that!'

'So then you found the man again?'

'Yeah, he'd been fat before but when we were walking toward him they were commenting on all his rolls - he was wearing a bright green swimming costume or something, and he looked *massive*, just standing there with his eyes shut!'

'His eyes were closed?'

'Yeah, so he didn't see us until we were right in front of him, *and* he was smiling!'

'What happened next then?'

'My brother was just scaring him a bit, but he was being right cocky! Then this massive paedophile turned up...'

'Sorry?'

'A paedophile!'

'How do you know he was a paedophile?'

'He was wearing these white trousers, *proper* giveaway!'

'Okay...that's not...'

'And there was a bit of a scrap, I think he *crapped* himself - the fat one - it *stunk*, then a few others appeared and we got a bit of a slapping actually, so we legged it! My Da was fuming with me when we got home that *I'd* not told the others about all his mates, but I hadn't seen *anyone* when I first met him!'

'Okay, that's *it* though? Nothing else later on?'

'No we stayed indoors, watched a film, drank what we *had* got hold of, and went to bed later, like just before midnight!'

'Okay, my colleague is going to take your address so we can speak to your brother…'

'He's away fishing with me Dad!'

'…then you can get on your way…*don't* hang around asking people to break the law for you!'

The officer stood and looked out across the narrow pond, toward the boating lake where he'd watched them leave under the canopy of trees. His eyes panned left toward the estate where the two of them had found Gary's body. Far off, as if under water, he heard running steps and a muffled voice.

'I *said*, is there CCTV?'

'Nope.'

Chapter 17: Friday, 20:45

'I miss Tom!'
'Who the fuck is Tom?'
'He was an old friend I had!'
'Foz, Gaz, Chris...Tom...we're not ninety, we shouldn't have this many people taken too soon from us!'
Remember Robin, from school?'
'Yeah…'
'He took his own life when we were in our *twenties*, you know!'
'Did he?'
'Yeah, before social media filtered news like that to everyone.'
'That's *so* fucking young.'
'His lass split up with him, I think.'
'That's no reason - but I bet it's the reason for so many. You're not defined by who you're with.'
'I definitely wouldn't want to be defined by David right now!'
'I've been visiting with Foz's Ma, you know lads!', said Hughesy.
'Have you?'
'We called in last week and she said…'
'*Foz* had been there?'
'Yeah! Dave nearly rang the white coats, *then* we saw the flowers.'
'Someone needs to explain what's going on.'
'Sorry, yeah so what Mickles mentioned is that I took her some flowers - I've been around *regularly* since the night of nicky nocky.'
'Michael!', said Michael, as he and Dave walked over to a wall a fair few yards away.
'Why?'
'Literally broke my heart seeing her like that!'
'Figuratively!'
'Whatever. Some days she knows I'm me and wants to hear stories about us as teenagers, some days she accuses me of stealing Foz's ashes, there's times when she just

stares blankly like she's never seen *this* face in her whole life…'

'And there's times she thinks *you're* him?'

'Yeah…they're the worst for me but I think the best for her! I just go along with it; is that bad? I don't instigate it or call her mam or anything, but when she thinks he's me I just carry on the conversation.'

'Wow!'

'Her eyes change, from friendly enough to this look of, I don't know what, maybe pride, love, adoration, maternal in some way.'

'That's *lovely* mate.'

'That's fucked up!'

'Yeah, when I leave I'm always torn between both your opinions!'

'Someone nip in and check if that food's ready yet!'

'You think Dave's okay?'

'Looks it!'

'Well, physically yeah, but mentally it looks like his missus is giving him a *beatdown*!'

'Hissus!'

'You know something else, that Mrs Forrester has told me?'

'What mate?'

'He had depression for years, and even tried to do it twice before!'

'*What*?'

'Are you *serious*?'

'Why didn't I know this?'

'That's what she said, and it was when she was talking to *me* so I think that was her lucid, clear thoughts.'

'Why would he have kept that from *us*?'

'It seems we all kept things from each other, things that somehow interfered with what we thought perceptions of us should be.'

'Like what?'

'Dave, for one. Cookie's emotions…'

'I don't wanna see Cookie's tail like Rose's hand in Titanic, sliding down the glass!'

'Rank!'

'Kev's bowel problems, Foz's issues with depression, Gaz still living at home - there's lots of examples.'

'But we relied on each other, we could have *told* each other.'

'But we *didn't*, did we.'

'Why not?'

'You've *never* told us about this Tom mate that you lost!'

'He was an old friend, that's all, on MySpace!'

'Was he kind of looking back over his shoulder on his picture?'

'Yeah, did *you* know him?'

'You're a dweeb! In this age of lockdowns we need to open up more, I think!'

'I think, lads, that it just wasn't socially acceptable to open up or admit failure or ask for help when *we* were growing up.'

'There's a lot more people to talk to nowadays, online as well, help is *everywhere*.'

'If you seek it! Not if you keep it all inside, not if you can't even tell *your* friends.'

'And Foz died a few months ago - all that help existed.'

'But he grew up *without* it, thinking real men don't ask, didn't he!'

'Does that *matter*?'

'I think it does! I think in twenty years there'll be gangs of fortysomethings sitting in parks and outside kebab shops saying goodbye to friends and waffling on about how when *they* were growing up men were taught to be men!'

'Same as us?'

'Exactly, and when we were the teenagers I bet there were blokes our age now losing friends and caveating it with the same bullshit *'men don't talk'* crap. It's fucking endless.'

'Take a second mate to breathe…'

'No, I don't need to. We need to stop waiting, and start making a difference. The whole fucking world is too *busy* being offended and mindful, fuck off and be angry! You lot said earlier that you felt anger and I get that but it should be outward anger, not internal, it's the only way we stop losing people that *can* be saved. If every bastard death from suicide was falling off a cliff instead, and happened because someone's fingertips had just slipped away from safety, we'd lean further forward! We'd stretch every sinew to hold on! We aren't doing enough at all, it's all there - the professionals and the desire and the twatting advice and the friends and family and all the support in the world but men do not get it, because...*because...*'. Lee tailed off.

'Because they need to learn that from a *very* early age', added Bucky.

'And that's only going to happen in schools isn't it! It's batshit crazy that schools don't already teach mental health stuff!'

'Schools, yeah, but more broadly it has to be a fundamental part of every child's upbringing! Schools can't do it alone. They're not equipped!'

'They try to', added Knacker. 'I've seen the kids doing home learning and it seems to get shoehorned into coaching sessions but it's a cursory mention written by someone with no clue how to deliver it.'

'I've overheard that stuff, too', said Hughesy, 'and it's usually a case of whoever makes the resources isn't trained in it, and whacks them together and sends them out the morning they're being delivered.'

'At least they're *trying*, I suppose?'

'Bad attempts actually turn the kids off more than no attempt. You wouldn't want History lessons written by someone who hasn't studied any of it, so it *shouldn't* be the case with mental health awareness!'

'Here's Kev with the grub!'

'All I'm getting at is that my kids, and yours, and Marie's, and their little rainbow kid, are all going to have pythagoras, and enjambment, and dates of battles and locations of glaciers in their heads when they could have had a session a week, or even month, on how to recognise the *signs* of struggle, *who* to speak to, *how* to speak to them, *why* to speak up...you get it?'

They all stood and nodded.

-

'So, it was what? A *cry for help*, an escape from your *boring* life? What?'

'None of that. I told Hughesy, and he *was* trying to talk me out of it, that I'm nearly forty and everything is so safe and perfect that I wanted to just be stupid, once more! I hadn't told them about the adoption process - they just found out I'm gay!'

'By the sounds of it, they knew years before *you* did!'

'Well, yeah okay - but I've just changed my opinion of what their opinion is of me.'

'Glad you're back to making full sense again. Are you sure you're alright though? That was some fall!'

'I can't believe I was in a *tree* - I've never been the tree-climbing kind.'

'Okay, stereotype, you *are* perfect you know, you don't need to be dangerous, we are about to do the scariest thing known to man together!'

'I *know*. Sorry for scaring you, and I'm a little sore but fine, yes.'

'Okay, well turn around, your *very* sensible friends are signalling us to go!'

Dave turned, and along the wall outside the kebab shop shone seven shiny white arses in the streetlight. To their right, Knacker was drinking a donner.

Chapter 18: Friday, 21:00

'Nice to see you get your big bum out and be silly, Cookie!'

'Ha yeah - sorry, I know I'm being the most serious one here but I've got so much going on that I feel like I need to put Gaz to rest in *my* head before I can deal with anything or anyone else.'

'Well, you can share the burden, right?'

'Yeah mate, I know. I *do* know. Thought you were off the bad stuff?'

'Since the diagnosis I've been pretty good, but I'm scared!'

'Scared?'

'Yeah, just...I know how unhealthy I am. I've got to get the jab and I'm in the same category for it as the over seventy-fives. What a kick in the teeth. Sorry son, you're a walking timebomb and you're made of that much ketchup that you've doubled your age as well as your width!'

'Haha at least you can laugh about it.'

'Have to.'

'Nobody has *ever* stood up for me like you did on nicky nocky night mate; I hope you know that. When you're being down on yourself just remember you're one brave bastard!'

'I've actually felt different since, you know. I know it's all in jest but the years of fat jokes and insults must have been like an invisible cloak or cloud or whatever - I've really put my foot down at home and been really assertive with the woman...she loves it!'

'Bet she does!'

'Mitch lad, didn't hear you catching up.'

'Been right behind you the whole time...not that *anyone* would have been able to see me!'

'There we go, back to normality.'

'Just kidding - this diabetes thing *really* worrying you then?'

'You really want to know?'

'Of course - we aren't just here for the good times.'

'When do we have *those*?'

'Okay, so the Doc has said I've got diabetes but it's coupled with high cholesterol, *obviously*, and high blood pressure, again pretty easy to see, and that I'm in quite a bad way - might result in heart attack or stroke, stuff like that.'

'Shit man, I thought diabetes meant you couldn't have more than one Mars Bar!'

'I just thought it was The Million Dollar Man's surname!'

'I used to wait until I was home on me todd, and just blast Sheer Heart Attack, the album, on vinyl while eating whatever I could find. The irony wasn't missed but I didn't care enough about myself. Now, I might have any number of complications.'

'My grandad had arthritis really bad, and I remember him saying *something* about diabetes, but I might be wrong', queried Cookie

'It definitely causes nerve pain, it seems to be able to affect allsorts. Anyway, I'm trying to eat healthily, but mainly just a *lot* less!'

'You tell that to the kebab you did like a shot of tequila!'

'That must be why they put a quarter of a lemon in with it!'

'Yeah, I broke lads, but that's the first thing since Dicky's car that's gone off piste!'

'Dicky's gone off pissed?'

'In his car?'

'He's not even here!'

'You're a pair of wankers, you know that!'

Chapter 19: Friday, 21:15

'I'm going to Gaz's!'
'Why?'
'Going to speak to his Da again - I want to know what *he's* hiding!'
'I'll go with Hughesy', said Cookie.
'Me too', added Knacker.
'Should we *all* come?'
'Naw mate, that might be a bit much turning up at his door!'
'As though you arriving with Earthquake and Typhoon isn't going to be scary?'
'Oy, I'm not *that* fat!', said Cookie.
'I'm not *that* slim!', added Knacker.
'It's just up here, I think, then we'll come back around the top way and meet you back at the VG.'
'Okay, see you soon.'
'Keep an eye out mind!'
'We will, we will!'
The group split in two, with Lee opting to follow Cookie, Knacker and Hughesy as they stayed on the main road and headed up the bank past the school entrance on their left. The others, including Hedz and Michael, turned left and went back through the canopy of trees with the schoolyard on their right, emerging back out onto the boating lake.
'That's where I was? Up *there*?'
'Yeah mate, you were going off it tweeting and that!'
'Which is weird because you've only just joined Facebook!'
'I don't get it?'
'You will when you join Twitter as well! Can you please learn that a hashtag is a symbol!'
'What is it?'
'It looks like a drunk noughts and crosses game - you need to stop writing hashtag on Facebook mate.'
'What's he doing?'
'I'll add you, Hedz!'
'You better not!', whispered Michael.

'He's putting a picture on and writing some shit like, I dunno, 'great time at the park, hashtagslide hashtagsunshine hashtagmylove'.

'What, writing the word?'

'Yep!'

'Well, I didn't know!'

'Haha Dave, man!'

'Hashtagmoron.'

'Piss off the lot of you! Hashtagheteros!'

I can't believe you're okay after that fall mind?'

'I just feel like I've tripped…'

'You *did*!'

'I can't believe you did LSD like, mate.'

'Me neither!', huffed Michael.

'You had a good, quick trip as well - I remember my first back in the day', said Kev. As they wandered around the edge of the boating lake, Bucky pulling the wheelbarrow behind him so it looked from the front as though he were holding two wine bottles by their necks, Kev recounted the first of two stories.

'We were all up at the cem and Hedz brought some of those yellow smileys for me, Foz, Gaz and him to try. I can't speak for them but it was shit. Or I thought anyway! Night passed, nothing. Walked home, back when we thought the cem was miles away as well, *nothing*. I had some food, frozen meal, and went up to my room. *Still* nothing.'

'If this is just going to end up being a story about you having a tug, we don't need to hear it!'

'Don't make out I'm some sort of depraved deviant!'

'Sorry, mate.'

'So if you all recall I had this black bedroom, and all the bed, wardrobes, cupboards, the lot were built into the walls and that, yeah? Yeah, good! Now me Mam had that done when I was about ten, and *all* the handles were bright white with…'

'Garfield on!'

'Yes! Each pair was Garfield in a different pose, and we never changed them. They're in the attic now; me Da keeps everything! I was like fifteen, sixteen, with fucking Garfield door handles all over a room covered in FHM posters! So…I was *about* to have a wank…'

'Depraved!'

'Deviant!'

'…whatever, I was a teenage boy on rollerblades, nobody else was going to touch it! When I see a movement…just little at first, in the dark, then another, but it's not moving around the room it's fixed in place, on one of the handles!'

'Garfield?'

'*Garfieldssssss*! All the little ginger bastards started moving and then gradually came in time with each other doing this manic dance routine! It was *unreal* - I did get wrong next day for having smeared lasagne on all the cupboards, but I still don't think that was me - one of the best things *ever*! That's the only reason I did acid the second time!'

'Sounds pretty cool, man!'

'Yep, best beat off ever!'

'You *still* had a wank?'

'Kev, that's like bestiality or something, pal!'

'You tell me that you would stop just because there were twenty imaginary cartoon cats dancing the macarena in your bedroom?'

'I wouldn't start!'

They crossed the small metal bridge separating the main boating lake from the long, narrow pool by the shop again, heading for their spot on the grass. They had hovered a moment during Kev's story to look for the police car in the shop car park, and then continued.

Chapter 20: Friday, 21:20

'What are we going to say?'
'Just want answers from the vile old twat!'
'Who's doing the talking?'
'I will, after our conversation the other day!'
'Okay, ring the bell then Cookie!'
Cookie went to, then stopped. Hughesy knocked on the door instead.
'PTSD?'
'Something like that.'
They waited, then knocked again, louder.
'Lights are on.'
'Gaz's were but that never meant anyone was home!'
'Might have left them on and gone out?'
'They're flickering - it's the TV that's on!'
Hughesy knocked a third time, louder still and for longer. The light came on near the door, blinds twitched and then an outline of a person appeared through the bevelled glass, turning the key.
'Might just crack the cunt', whispered Knacker.
'Woah Knacker, not like you!'
'Never hated *anyone* as much as this…'
The door began to open.
'Can I help?'
'Oh, sorry love', muttered Hughesy. 'We've got the wrong house I think.'
'No, I don't think you have.'
'Really? What?'
'Sorry it took so long to answer; at first I thought it would just be the local kids playing Knock Down Ginger!'
'Nicky Nocky…'
'Shhh, man Lee! We came along to *hopefully* speak to Gaz's Dad?'
'Do you think that's wise? He was really shaken up after the way *you* went on at the bookmakers - couldn't get in the car fast enough!'
'*You* were there?'
'Sorry, but who *are* you?'

'Melissa. I look after Cliff.'
'Another parent with a name!'
'Can we speak to Cliff?'
'Why? What can that achieve?'
'We want to know what happened to Gaz!'
'He was out with *you* that night, not here.'
'He came back *here* though, didn't he! The police said his wallet and watch were here.'
'I don't think he took them out that night. He only had a few things here anyway, and he hadn't mentioned coming back here - he'd talked a *lot* about meeting up with you all!'
'Where would he have gone back *to*?'
'*His* flat.'
He didn't still live *here* with his Dad?'
'He was nearly forty! No, he didn't - he stayed over a couple of nights a week when I wasn't here and to save money on the on-call provision.'
'But why did the police say he'd been back here and left his stuff?'
'And when I spoke to 'Cliff' he was *bragging* about the life insurance! Do you know what *kind* of man he is?'
'Was! Yes, I do. He's talked about it a lot, and how he should have got help when Gary was a child but he didn't know how - it's *his* life insurance!'
'It is now, yeah!'
'No, literally the insurance was on his own life - a policy that paid out a lump sum for terminal illness before death, to set affairs in order.'
'Terminal illness?', asked Lee
'He has days or weeks left - he was trying to pay everything off for Gary after he'd gone but now he just wants to blow it all!'
'I'm so sorry - I completely misunderstood the other day!'
'I think it's understandable given *your* recollection of Cliff, but people change! Hearing him at the funeral, without context...'
'*You* were the woman at the crem? Of course!'
'Gary was a lovely man - it was heartbreaking.'
'I still don't understand the wallet and wat...'

'Here!' Cliff opened the door fully to reveal he had been standing behind it. 'Take them. He didn't come back here! Because of you, he *never* will!'

'Sorry, it's nobody's fault!'

As Melissa closed the door, and they heard Cliff begin to cough uncontrollably, Cookie said 'it's *somebody's'* under his breath. Hughesy lifted the lid on the shoebox slightly, then turned to the others.

'We have to get back to the VG, right fucking *now*!'

Chapter 21: Friday, 21:30

'...and she stood up *in* the court, to the judge and *everyone*, and said 'set my boy free, you know how easily someone's *ear* comes off when you bite it' didn't she!'

'Haha *really*? Wow!'

'Maternal love that - defend *everything*!'

'Not from mine...mine was *attack* everything! Especially me!'

'Really, mate? I didn't know this.'

'It was weird, but I couldn't see it as abuse when I was younger - take Gaz, he's coming to us with his arm in a sling, or a black eye - I couldn't turn around and say, the same happens to me, but with *words*.'

'Especially as a *boy*!'

'Exactly, how emasculating would that be to be bullied by a woman - and I felt like I was the bad one because all your Ma's were lush, even Foz's before she checked in to the cuckoo's nest, so to break whatever maternal shite is supposed to be natural...I always believed I'd done it somehow.'

'I don't mean this as it sounds, but can't think of a better way to put it - I'm really *enjoying* all opening up to each other!'

'Not in the way Dave would like!'

'*I've* ruined him for you lot!', retorted Michael.

'I get that, and not enjoying but *appreciating* maybe?'

'You know', said Hedz, 'I think you're probably all looking back, like I know I have, and thought we could have been more supportive by knowing and telling each other stuff, but don't overlook the fact that by being mates that *was* supportive, that was the escape some of us may have needed.'

'You mean we didn't have to know what each other were going through to help each other through it?'

'Precisely that! But that's not to say we shouldn't have been able to speak to each other back then; I've been investing in our old school - obviously they think I'm a different kind of businessman - and what you lads were saying, and what Lee was ranting about, back at the kebab shop, is something I am absolutely going to push for.'

'I want to apologise', said Michael. 'I had you wrong!'

'No need, we all attribute stereotypes to people, don't we? Now stay back, you've got the bad Aids!'

'Can I ask something?'

'Yeah, Bucky?'

'What's your *second* story, Kev?'

'Oh, I was hoping we'd get back to *that*!'

'Right then...so we were up at the big little park and it was a few...'

'Lads!'

'Ooh, how was it?'

'He's dying!'

'Cookie, what the fuck did *you* do!'

'He's been dying a while! Listen to Hughesy!'

'They all stopped chuckling, realising how seriously Lee and Knacker were staring at them.

'What's going on?'

'Long story, but most of it can wait...'

'Like mine!', butted in Kev.

'...we've got a box of Gaz's stuff, his wallet and watch, shrapnel...'

'Right?'

'*This* is his watch!'

'He *never* went home!'

'Nope, well he never went to his Da's place, he didn't still live there after all, we were right.'

'Then does that mean the young fella from the funeral...'

'The one we saw in the shop earlier...'

'That's what we think as well.'

'Fuck...we *have* to find him!'

'How?'

'This is what we think...', said Hughesy, sitting down and placing the box on the grass in front of him. On top, he laid the silver metal Tag Heuer watch with the clasp strap.

Chapter 22: Friday, 22:00

'You're going to have to explain the craic with the watch, Lee', pressed Hedz.

'We dressed up in nineties clothes on the night of Foz's send-off, the night Gaz was attacked.'

'Why?'

'We thought it would be a fun way of remembering him, mine and Bucky's idea - Kev found Adidas poppers, Bucky had a colour changing t-shirt, Dave got his order messed up and was in seventies fancy dress...'

'Bloody hell, what about you?'

'I was wearing white chinos...'

'You came as a Colombian druglord?'

'Thank you! Everyone else said...'

'Who was also a kiddyfiddler?'

'Fuck's sake. Anyway, Gaz was in jeans and a plain black t-shirt, but he had on the classic Casio and everyone thought *his* was better...'

'Top notch nineties garb!'

'So the copper said at Cookie's party that Gaz's watch was at his Dad's, and we all thought that meant *he'd* been back *there*. Also, there was this lad at the crem and Kev and Dave saw him in the shop earlier wearing the same watch.'

'But at that point they thought Gaz's was accounted for?'

'Exactly! Kid did a runner too, which makes more sense now.'

'So what are *we* doing, hoping he comes back past?'

'Yeah, we still don't know who *he* is!'

'And we're watching for a gang of kids as well? That what Cookie said?'

'Yeah mate, sorry you've got involved in all this, you can go if you want you know!'

'Naw, I liked Gaz!'

'Good customer?'

'At school yeah - not one of mine these days.'

'Right. So Cookie saw one of these kids we had a fight with...'

'Why the fuck were you fighting with *kids*?'

'I'm saying kids, but they were late teens, older than we were when we knocked about here. A couple of them were big as well, one *almost* the size of Cookie!'

-

'How would this kid have *got* Gaz's watch though, if he's a relative or something?', asked Mitch.

'Dunno, Kev saw it though, I was looking at the telly behind the counter - first I knew the lad was off like a shot and I just ran after Kev. Last time I was in the VG I came out and Knacker and Lee were getting a kicking - felt like deja vu!'

'Dave ja vu!'

'Gay ja vu!'

'Oh, yours was *better*!'

'Dickheads. You think Michael's alright with Knacker and Hughesy?'

'Wey aye...but why didn't he want to be with you?'

'Said he *wants* to get to know you lot better.'

'What a *freak*!', replied Mitch.

'Everything there is to know about me is worn on my sleeve!', added Bucky.

'Hope you remember what these twats looked like as well, remember me and Bucky were over by the boaty when you had the scrap.'

'I saw a couple of them properly, the ones I was barneying with along with Lee. I don't think I saw the faces of the two that were left on Knacker while Cookie brayed the big one. I'd recognise *him* though. I think someone called him Shane or something at some point.'

'Right, so between us we'd recognise possibly maybe just half of them, perhaps?'

'Good lookouts, us!'

-

'So, how have we ended up here, then? Dave told me his jumper had been ruined but it's not until tonight I've *really* known why.'

'Oh, that tank top! What a pleasure it was to see it bloodied and gone!'

'To be honest, Mick...'

'It's *Michael*!'

'...yeah, it was all my fault I guess. I was a bit of a prick to this lad and then his mates came down and had a go. We all ended up scrapping, except Bucky and Mitch who'd gone ahead with *this* bloody thing, and Hughesy and Gaz were in the shop I think. Oh, and Kev was having a shit in the bushes!'

'He what?'

'He's better *now*.'

'Now he just masturbates to dancing cartoon characters?'

'Eh? What the fuck happened when we were at Gaz's?'

'Kev can tell you later.'

'So do you really think these young people would have stabbed Gaz though?'

'Don't want to, but yeah.'

'I want to have more faith in childhood than that. Can't think of anyone else though, so at least we can rule them out by talking to them!'

'Why would kids carry knives? I can never understand anyone doing that, least of all young people!'

'Fear, I reckon. They are so scared that they may be a victim that they take one, then it gives them an excuse to use it instead of walking away. Especially part of a group!'

'It's *insane*. Because they had one someone else will think *they* need one, and so on.'

'Nobody ever got stabbed by someone who *didn't* have a knife!'

'Genius. You should go into writing slogans!'

'Am I wrong?'

'No...I get your point!'

'That a joke?'

'Was it funny?'

'No.'

'Then no.'

-

'Cookie mate?'

'Yeah?'

'Are you aware that we are all standing in the shadows, watching for teenagers, after ten o'clock at night?'

'I am Kev, I am.'

'And that strategically placed or not, we *still* look like absolute planks.'

'Point?'

'If that kid *was* watching us earlier, he's told his mates and they 'ain't coming back!'

'It *was* him.'

'And whoever the guy from the funeral was, he's long gone!'

'Right.'

'So I think we're better off coming back tomorrow, like you said, and starting over. Those police will have scared them off too!'

'Right.'

'You listening, mate?'

'Yeah yeah, you're probably right but I feel like we're giving up.'

'No, we're just getting ready. Having a better shot at it.'

Cookie whistled, and they all gathered outside the shop, on a scratched and mouldy wooden bench, under the manic tangerine grin.

'Here, tomorrow, eight o'clock when it's already getting darker, *deal*?'

'Deal mate.'

'Yep!'

'Okay, lads!'

'Later!'

They all set off in their various directions, or got into their cars and drove away. Just over the hill, where they had been sat earlier in the evening and had discussed where they could best hide to watch for the man from the funeral and the young lad who had been watching them from the shop while the policeman had talked to Hedz, lay both the people they were trying to find.

Because 'they' was one person.

Chapter 23: Saturday, 20:00

'Where's Human traffic?'

'Hedz has other commitments; he's running a youth club he said, to keep kids off the street on a weekend.'

'He's the *exact* opposite of what you expect a drug dealer to be!'

'Well, no - he still *deals* the drugs! I get the ethics and I see his logic, he's clearly trying to make a difference as well, but it's *still* a crime. He's *still* a criminal even if he's been wrapped in gold!'

'Fair enough - where's Mike?'

'He's staying home lads, and I've *only* come out to let you know I'm *not* staying!'

'That's not why you 'came out'!'

'I will miss the intelligent banter, Bucky, but I wanted to say this to all of you face-to-face rather than by text…'

'Yeah?'

'Go on?'

'I am hopefully going to be a dad and I cannot put myself in ridiculous situations that might jeopardise that! I love you all, I genuinely do, and this has nothing to do with Foz or Gaz or not wanting to be with you lads...it's just the *right* thing to do.'

For a few eternal seconds, the other seven stared silently.

'I'm sor…', muttered Dave before they all embraced him.

'Don't be sorry mate, there's *nothing* to apologise for!'

'You big gay bear - we don't think less of you, you know!'

'I think better of you *actually*!'

'Thanks, lads!'

'We better be fucking invited to the bairn's christenings and birthdays and all that shite though!'

'Absolutely! You're invited to our house any time as well, just maybe not *all* of you at once!'

'Giz another hug lads - we love you too Davey boy, and tell Mickatron we can't wait to see you as parents!'

'You know it's Michael, right? You do hear him keep correcting you all?'

'Yeah!'

'Defo!'
'We're just taking the *Mickey*!'
'Knobs!'
'Speaking of, Knacker are you pleased to see me?'
'Bye then lads, be careful!'
'Later, Dave!'
'No mate, it's this bloody monitor!'
'Heart monitor, Ted Diabetes?'
'No, I told Cookie I had a few baby things for him. This is a wireless, 4G, battery-powered monitor - it connects straight to an app on your phone and you can save and watch wherever it's placed. I charged it and checked the app worked today when I got it down from the loft!'
'Holy shit!'
'It's a pretty cool device, yeah!'
'No', said Mitch, 'holy shit, *you* got into the *loft*?'
'I'm losing weight lads!'
'What have you brought that for?'
'I said I'd give it you, can stick it in the car in a bit.'
'You are looking better like Knacker, in general.'
'I've started getting a bit frisky with the woman as well - just feel more energetic!'
'Good lad - I'd be all over that wife of yours like Ethopians on a Big Mac!'
'Well, she's actually been putting me off - while we're at it!'
'How *could* she?'
'Thanks to you twats, and I appreciate you were *trying* to make me look cool, she thinks 'Knacker' is a compliment because of how brave I am! The daft bat keeps screaming 'ooh, Knacker' and I've got to chase the image of some cunt calling me an overweight testicle out of my head *mid-thrust*!'
'Hahaha sorry *Mountain*!'
'Bunch of bastards!'
'You could have said you'd lied to her.'
'You would have stitched me up on purpose then!'
'True. Are *you* staying?'
'Yeah, definitely.'

'Anyone else want to bow out? No shame, like Dave said, we've all got commitments and can't risk things getting messy!'

'I'm in two minds, honestly lads. I'm gonna stay for Gaz, not because I don't want to go.'

'Okay. Then what we need to do is take up the positions we were in last night, keep our eyes pee...I don't believe it!'

'What is it Victor Meldrew?'

'That lad's just gone in the shop - don't turn around. He wasn't looking this way.'

'How'd you know it was him?'

'Yellow Adidas jacket!'

'The lad from the crem was wearing a yellow jacket in the shop...wait, I'm confused.'

'Was the lad from the fight the *same* lad that you saw with Gaz's watch on, Kev?'

'I don't know!'

'Why don't you know?'

'I didn't *see* the fight, did I?'

'You were having a shit! Fuck me...'

'Well, did *you* recognise him at the service?'

'I was hiding behind Knacker, from the priest fella!'

'Cookie?'

'No, I was stopping Bucky from slagging off Gaz's Da, wasn't I!'

'Knacker?'

'I was eating, then that crazy monk went bonkers at me...I didn't notice *him*!'

'Monk, priest, vicar, pastor...'

'What *are* we saying here? The kid who Knacker had a go at, he then got his friends and started on us, then later *killed* Gaz, went to his *funeral* and kept his watch? It doesn't add up!'

'Mitch, Bucky, you're probably the fastest, get 'round the other side of the VG will you? Lee, with me, rest of you *stay* here!'

'Eh? Why?'

'He's just a kid, and there's a slim chance he's done nothing wrong, but it's looking *very* unlikely! Still, seven of us can't descend on him!'

Cookie and Lee started jogging toward the entrance, as Mitch and Bucky were already vanishing behind the shop, having sprinted across the metal bridge.

Chapter 24: Saturday, 20:15

'How's your dad doing?'
'Alright, yeah.'
'Tell him I was asking after him, okay pet!'
'Will do, cheers.'

He left the shop and turned slightly to the left, beginning to head toward the cut into the estate when he heard someone behind him.

'Hello *again*.'

Turning, he replied shakily, 'I don't know you!'

'Sure you do. Wait there a second, we need a word.'

'Fuck off', he shouted, as he turned to run, spotting Mitch coming from around the shop to his left. He zagged right and broke into a sprint, turning back as he reached the alleyway well ahead of the three old men.

'Old twats!', he shouted, sticking two fingers up. As he turned back, a purple, tattooed arm flashed through the air and he felt his legs disappear from underneath his body.

-

'You think they're the *most* logical, sensible ones to be going over and talking to that kid?'

'Yeah, of course. What do you think they'd do? *Torture* him?'

'Well, while we're waiting, the second time I took a tab was late November, probably ninety-six, about a month after...'

'The Gar-feel!'

'Very clever, like what you've done there, Hughesy!'

'Hello again, chaps. Why is it you are back here, in the same spot I asked you to leave just yesterday?'

'Do you always creep about?'

'Are you always either stoned, drunk or mesmerised by the Happy Shopper?'

'Well...'

'I'm not here to move you on, don't worry. Nice to see there's no alcohol or dodgy smells in the air today. I spoke to someone yesterday and I'm waiting on catching up with some people I'd like to get some more information from, but I wanted you to know I am doing everything I can, and will get to the bottom of this.'

'You sound like Dave!'

'Dave is trying to get to the bottom of this?'

'Dave is just trying to get to the bottom!'

'I'm sorry, are you making a homophobic comm…'

'Good to hear. We appreciate your efforts.'

'I'm telling you as well because I'm sure you are aware that Cliff became very ill late last night and is now in hospital, unlikely to ever come back home. You are the *only* people who seem to care what happened now.'

'We will do *whatever* it takes to get to the…to find out what happened!'

'That's my worry. The only issue would be if other events started interfering, getting in the way, you know.'

'Can't imagine *that* happening mate.'

'Your friend not here? Chris's big brother?'

'No, he's not tonight. Just us three actually!'

'Okay…take care, and contact us if you need to.'

'Will do.'

'I hope they're not doing anything *stupid'*, whispered Knacker as the officer walked away behind them.

-

'Wake up…'

'…'

'Wake up, you little cunt!'

'…huh, what…'

'Shut up and listen!'

He looked around, and knew he was still near the shop. They were in a garden - lots of houses in a few streets had been bought back by the council, boarded up and were ready to be knocked down. They were building a coffee shop, little supermarket and a dentists or something. The Happy Shopper had been leafleting asking local residents to petition against it, but most thought it would add value to their own property. Besides, he remembered his Dad saying, it was a chain anyway nowadays, not like when they were little and it was part of the community. The biggest of them, the one who had dealt so easily with Sean, who everyone thought was the hardest lad in the area, was right in his face.

'What happened to our mate? The one who was stabbed?'

'The coppers were asking about that as well, and I swear it's got nothing to do with us!'

'Bull*shit*', said the one behind the giant.

'I know you, you're that *paedo*!'

'Fuck off!'

'Are you *not* a paedo?'

'Of course I'm not a fucking paedo!'

'Why've you kidnapped a kid then, hew?'

'Kidnap? This isn't *kidnap*…', laughed Bucky.

'What is it then? I'm not here of my own free will!'

Cookie, Mitch, Lee and Bucky seemed to take in the gravity of the situation.

'How old are you?', asked Mitch.

'Fourteen.'

'At fourteen, why are you starting trouble on the streets?'

'I'm *not*. I was trying to get *away* from it!'

'I mean last time, a couple of months ago, I know you remember outside the VG!'

'What's a *VG*?'

'The shop, son. Look, that night our friend was killed - someone we were best friends with from much younger than you are now. Gaz was killed, and *you* went to his funeral, and now you're…'

'*Gary's* funeral! I went to *Gary's* funeral, but I didn't know *he* was the one who got stabbed!'

'Why were you there?'

'How did you know him, then?'

They started to back away.

'I got community service last year, for knocking wing mirrors off, and I had to take part in this initiative where we went and painted fences around town. This old man, Cliff, started asking about what I'd done, and said he'd got some odd jobs needed doing if I kept out of *trouble*. He rang my dad and made sure it was all okay. Cliff got sick though, just when someone was being supportive like, and then Gary started coming around. He was *just* like his Dad, really supportive and listened, you know. He set me up with a paper round and said he would help me get an apprenticeship when I was leaving school.'

'Sorry, kid.'

'He made me sign up to this youth project - I'm just on my way back now. It gives *us* somewhere to go, you know. The night of that fight I was meant to be going there, then I had to get drink for my brother first, then all *that* happened.'

'Did you know someone was killed that night?'

'Yeah, I saw on Facebook, but *they* didn't know his name. I went around to see Cliff and Mel, that's his nurse now he's sick, sat me down and told me about Gary, but she didn't say *how* he died, just *when* the funeral was.'

'Fuck me. This is brutal.'

'Gary and Cliff had got me a shirt and trousers, and told me to always look smart, like when I went to get the paper round - seemed silly - so I wore them for the funeral. Didn't expect the po-po to be there! I was meant to sit with Mel but she was next to him!'

'Sorry I knocked you out, kid!'

'It's okay. I've had worser. I recognised your git fat friend at the crem place so I hid until you'd gone.'

'Why did you come back to attack our 'fat friend'?'

'I didn't *want* to. I got shouted at for not getting the drink and I said what had happened, then I got dragged back down there! I think your friend shit himself, you know - he pulled me down and it *stunk*!'

'It wasn't him.'

'Right. Sorry about Gary, he was *really* nice.'

'He was, yeah. We always thought he was called Gareth!'

'Until recently.'

'You seemed to know him *more* than we did!'

'Can I go?'

'Yeah.'

'Wait a sec...', Bucky held his hand up and the kid flinched, 'sorry, I was just wanting to ask when you got *your* watch?'

'A few weeks ago, maybe a couple of months, why?'

'Gaz had one!'

'Naw, his was a fancy silver one - this is just a cheap one off me Dad!'

Chapter 25: Saturday, 20:45

'Did you manage to steal Gaz while you were at his Da's place, then?'

'I didn't *steal* Foz you know', defended Hughesy.

'I know mate. I wonder what they've done with Gaz though?'

'Yeah, good point.'

'I'm real glad he didn't *still* live at home.'

'Yeah, but I can't believe he was helping take care of *his* old man!'

'I guess Gaz was just a better person than him, no matter what he put him through!'

'I couldn't do it, me. I'm not as good a person as Gaz was.'

'You know earlier, I was saying about my Mam?'

'Yeah - bullying *is* bullying mate - you could have said you know.'

'I know, it's not about that. I think I get where Gaz was coming from - when I had kids, I suddenly felt this urge to try and *include* her. I'd spent years trying to get away, always asking my dad if I could go and live with him, and then it's like, a switch - I think you become a parent and feel so much love that you can't comprehend *anyone* treating kids badly. I guess it distorted my view; she was a nasty woman, and despite *my* efforts, stayed that way. I should never have given her the chance.'

'You think Gaz's Da is still the same?'

'I dunno - he drank heavily didn't he, maybe it was that.'

'His nurse mentioned that he didn't know *how* to get the help he needed.'

'For me, that's an excuse, plenty people struggle without braying their bairns!'

'And my mam wasn't a drunk, she was a *dick*!'

'Haha'.

'When Gaz's Da dies, that's it for that family - all gone.'

'Do you think we come back?'

'I think *they* are!'

'Oh, how do lads!'

'Any luck?'

'Yeah, we found the lad. Bucky sparked him.'

'Thanos arm, should have just clicked your fingers!'

'What did he say then? I don't hear sirens so I'm guessing he isn't responsible, or his body isn't going to be found?'

'The first one...pretty messed up kid, but he seemed to have a genuine relationship with Gaz...and Cliff it seems!'

'We've been talking about Cliff's turnaround.'

'Better than Dave's reacharound!'

'He's not here to appreciate that, Mitch!'

'Bugger!'

'Or that!'

'So anyway, the kid was at the crem to say his goodbyes, nothing else. Him and his mates, well his big brother's mates, I don't get the impression he wants to be like them, they stayed home the rest of the night after we saw them off.'

'Are we no further forward, then?'

'Well, yeah, actually, I think we *are*!'

'Do you? You never said?'

'Been thinking walking back over', said Bucky, 'and I don't think we're done here yet.'

'Where?'

'The VG.'

Chapter 26: 1995

'Look at all this, lads - the world is our playground again and we will always be free to do what we want and go where we want to go!', shouted Gaz.

'Let's get drinking then!'

'Bucky and Mitch have gone to the shop to ask someone to go in!'

'As if we're trusting stoned Zig and Zag...'

'Haha classic!'

'I wish there was a way of getting in touch with Hedz, you know!'

'His number's in the book, we can run to mine and ring him?'

'You know what, lads?'

'What, Gaz?'

'I *love* you lot you know! You're my *real* family!'

'Oh, fuck off!'

'Gay as fuck!'

'Gay Gareth!'

'My name's not...'

'They're being stupid mate. *Some* of us just haven't matured yet! Right, go on Lee!'

With that, Lee, who had been holding his lighter alight and aloft for several minutes, let go of the switch and rammed the metal end into Cookie's hand, where the soft skin joins the thumb and finger!

'I don't care if we *never* mature! I just want to stay here, all of us together, out here on the grass all night!'

'Am I bollocks sleeping out with you when you're feeling all lovey-dovey!'

'Howay lads, I don't want to go *home*!'

'There's hours yet, man! Then we've got a few weeks and it'll be the summer holidays!'

'Dave and me's gonna run and ring Hedz', said Lee.

'It's under See-oh-ban, his Ma is Irish!'

'What the hell is a *see-oh-ban*?'

'It's pronounced Shevon, mate!'

'Nee wonder he has to get wasted!'

'Why *don't* you want to go home, Gaz?'
'I just...want to stay with you lot!

-

'What happened to you?'
'Fell off my bike!'
'Have you got a bike?'
'Well, I fell off a friend's bike!'
'We're your only friends!'
'Just a neighbour's bike, *okay*!'
'Okay, on the blob?'
'I'd be acting like I'd got the painters in if I'd broken me arm on the *first* day of the Summer holidays as well!'
'Look, it doesn't matter! Here', Gaz gave them a pen to write on his arm. 'At least we've got all this time together - whenever in our lives will we ever get the chance to stay off work or school for six weeks? This is our last shot!'
'What about next year?'
'We'll all have weekend jobs and that - I'm planning on going straight to work with me uncle!'
'You're *not* coming to college, Lee?'
'No, mate.'
'You can't break up the band!'
'Me neither', added Gaz.
'Why? You haven't got *any* family to go and work for!'
'No, but you call me Gaz the Spaz, lads. I get worse at home. I'm not clever enough to go to college.'
'There's courses to be PE teachers, you know!'
'Haha no, I wouldn't want to end up like Mr. Hardon!'
'Ooh, definitely not.'
'We won't all be going to the *same* college, you know, the ones that *are* going!'
'Won't we?'
'No, I'm going to QE, and I know Mitch is going to the god-botherer college!'
'They do a better engineering course!'
'Is it taught by a vicar though?'
'It's a priest, isn't it?'
'What's the difference?'
'I don't know, aren't they all the same?'

'If they're going bald, they're monks!'
'Imagine going bald!'
'You're *already* receding like, Lee!'
'Fuck off!'
'What do you think Foz and Dave are talking about? They've been over on the swings ages!'
'Probably Pee Fun Willies, knowing Dave!'
'Why's he not telling us?'
'About the willies?'
'About being gay!'
'No way is one of our mates a *homo*!'
'So what if he is?'
'But we've all been skinnydipping up the res together!'
'Oh yeah!'
'Being gay doesn't mean you are attracted to *every* male you see, or can't look away when there's a cock out! It's just like being straight!'
'I'm straight and I am attracted to every single female I see, and if there was even just a bit of sideboob I'd probably walk into traffic!'
'You're a slut though, Cookie!'
'Sluts are girls!'
'Yeah!'
'Don't think so - we'll ask these two, they're our cleverest representatives!'
'What you two been talking about?'
'Just plans, like, for the Summer!'
'Chilling on the swings!'
'You like to *swing*, Dave?'
'Yeah, it's relaxing…'
'Ask us what?', interjected Foz, taking the pen from Cookie and holding Gaz's arm.
'Tell Hughesy a slut is a girl!'
'I don't think so, it's anyone who's promiscuous, isn't it!'
'Who's what?'
'Promiscuous!'
'I'm definitely not a slut then - I don't do all that leather shit!'
'What? Promiscuous just means you sleep around!'

'I never go to *sleep* with them!'

'Fucking hell. A slut is anyone who shags about - get it! You are definitely a slut.'

'At least I'm not a slag!'

'No, I think…'

'Leave it, Knacker, leave him be. Too much thinking for one day.'

'Cheeky twat!'

'Lads, me and Foz were talking and we thought we could get a ghettoblaster, some tapes, as much drink as possible, and some green Hedz mate, and head up the cem one Saturday morning…'

'Obviously they've finished all the building work now, and haven't started using it, so we take tents and plenty batteries…'

'Wahey!'

'…for the ghettoblaster you pleb - and stay until the Sunday night. Just camp out like Gaz wanted to.'

'Lads, that sounds *awesome*!'

'It's such a *long* walk though!'

'Knacker, man - what can we do?'

'Grandad's got a wheelbarrow! We could roll the chubber up there!'

'Fuck you, I'm just saying!'

'And I'll need a hand putting my tent up!'

'Quite literally, Gaz!'

'No problem, we'll put yours up or you can share with someone.'

'When we doing this then?'

'I haven't got a tent!'

'And we're off on holiday next week - I don't wanna miss this though!'

'No we'll do it middle of August - everyone here then?'

'Yeah.'

'Yeah, man!'

'Sweet, dudes! Okay, where we heading now?'

'VG!'

'Ooh what a refreshing change!'

'Once we're old enough to drive I hope we never *ever* find

ourselves hanging about that fucking place again!'

As they walked, talking about plans for camping out, Mitch and Bucky suddenly broke into a sprint. The rest realised quickly, and began to run. A door opened, and a man in his fifties looked out, saw Gaz just about to run, having been reading his own arm, and proceeded to crack him in the face with a long stick.

-

'Where have *you* been? We've knocked on *every* day for you!'

'After that old fella hit me with the cane, my dad just wanted me to stay home.'

'Gaz...you can tell us *anything* you know!'

'What do you mean?'

'Well, last week you got twatted on the head by that bloke, right!'

'Yeah.'

'But it was just a long cut down your forehead - you can't expect us to believe that cut turned into all that *bruising*!'

'On the *opposite* side of your face!'

'Alright - bloody hell are you lot joining the police or something?'

'We'd never make good detectives, we're too easily distracted!'

'My little brother and his mate Zac think they're proper investigators, bless them.'

'Wanna be careful your Chrissy doesn't find your stash then, Hedz!'

'Right Gaz - *truth*!'

'Really?' Gaz looked from one face to the next, then back again around the circle they were sat in. 'Okay. I *didn't* fall off a bike. I *didn't* get all this from that bloke with the cane!'

'We know mate. It's *okay*.'

Gaz took a deep breath, and when he looked up he was crying. Lee put a hand on his shoulder, and urged him to go on. Then, like a dam breaking, words flowed out.

'I *didn't* break my leg on a horse when on holiday a couple of years ago. I *didn't* accidentally burn myself with the iron over that first Christmas we were at comp. I *didn't* lose all of my front teeth on a roundabout when we were in year four. I didn't *fall* or *bump* or *slip* or run into most of the things that I have said I did...'

'I'll *kill* him!', said Cookie.

'It's only when he's drunk! But that's been more and more recently! Last week I told him I'd got a clip when it wasn't even me, and *he* battered *me*!'

'For what?'

'For playing that game, for *not* running, for lying, for having *bad* friends - he said all of them but they were just excuses he was thinking of for why he was hitting me! I had to barricade my door!'

'Tell someone? We'll help you do it!'

'Go into *care*?'

'Or come and live with one of us?'

'I can't do that. My Mam left him, and I can't do that too!'

'Does he even love you?'

'I don't know, I think so. He's never been the kind to take me fishing, or camping, or to play football with me, but when he has been sober, he has been...okay...to be around.'

'Fuck, man!'

'I *know* what you're going through...'

'You live with your Ma! And there's never a mark on you!'

'Unless it's gravy stains!'

'Haha at least you're *trying* to sound *supportive* Knacker!'

'I do though', muttered Knacker to himself.

'Gaz mate, you can't live like this though - you have to do *something*!'

'Can I just forget about it when I'm with you lot? That's the best thing, for me.'

'Yeah, but...'

'That's the *best*! Thanks, lads. Can we talk about something else now though?'

'Erm...right, camping next weekend!'

'Do you like to *camp*, Dave?'

'Everyone got tents sorted?', interrupted Foz.

'I just need to borrow mine off a neighbour kid.'

'I'm sorted, yeah.'

'Me too!'

'I think we only need four, for the ten of us, if you're coming Hedz?'

'Lads, this Summer has been class - rights am I!'

'Glad I rang your Mam the first day?'

'Oh aye, but she still thinks you're a dickhead for calling her *Sleight-of-hands*, Lee!'

-

On Saturday morning, the 19th of August 1995, eleven figures traipsed along the side of the ring road around the top of the town. All uphill, they were visibly exhausted when they entered the cemetery and walked all the way to the far end, where there was a white stone building with pillars, and to the left of it you could look out across the whole town below. Tents and crates were thrown down, and someone was coughing wildly.

'That wheelbarrow idea seems better now', wheezed Knacker!

'Next time we have this much booze to shift, we'll steal my Grandad's!'

'Deal!'

'You need to stop the smoking, mate!'

'I'm alright...it's bloody *boiling*!'

'Did anyone bring suncream?'

'No, mother!'

'I did!'

'That one bottle won't go far, Knacky!'

'It's for my massive face and top chin!'

'Haha - *top chin*!'

'I say we don't rest up - let's get the tents up and then we can be chilling by elevenish?'

'Who's being Mammy now?'

'I agree - if we have a drink or a smoke, we'll end up sleeping on top of the flat tents tonight.'

'Get the tunes on at least!'

'You've got a ghettoblaster? This is *so* cool lads!'

'Why are you here, Dicky?'

'Dave wanted my tent, I wanted to camp out, voila!'

'Well, you get to share with Dave!'

'Why's that a *bad* thing?'

'He snores', butted in Foz.

As Waterfalls by TLC began to resound off the pillars behind them, they all set to work putting up their tents. Within five minutes, Dicky was done.

'What the fuck? How've you done that?'

'Dave is good at *erecting* things!'

'I did it!', said Dicky. 'Camp out most weekends, even before the Summer!'

'Wanna do mine?'

'Waterfalls...Unchained *bastard* Melody...what is this, Bucky?'

'It's recorded off the radio - I forgot to bring the tapes and this was in the deck.'

'Load of shite! Wish we had a telly!'

'Oh 'cos everyone just carries a telly around in their pocket don't they!'

'One day they might!'

'Don't be so fucking stupid!'

'Tyson fight is on tonight, that's all!'

'Oh, so you not only want a telly, but *also* a satellite dish?'

'You've made your point, Mitch, don't be a prick.'

'Wait while I check my jacket, there's a hole in the pocket and things sometimes slip through the lining!'

'Knob off!'

-

'Wish Don't Forget Your Toothbrush was still on lads, remember what it was like up here last year on a night?'

'Yeah, looked *class*.'

'After what I've drank and smoked today, I would not want the whole town to be strobing! I'd vom!'

'You not want this Aftershock/Mad Dog shitmix then?'

'Hell no, but it's nice to see the flask of death getting a run out.'

'It's been a lush day, lads - really one of the *best* days of my life!'

'That's 'cos you've been *safe* mate.'

'I think I'll sleep really well tonight, having been with you guys, knowing I'll wake up with you tomorrow.'

'Someone take Gaz to bed before he sets us all off!'

'I just love you lot…'

'There we go!'

'I'm still willing to kill your dad if you want! I've been accepted into the Marines lads, so I'll learn a few tricks then come back and kick his lips off!'

'When do you go?'

'September.'

'Will you be an assassin like that Desperado we watched?'

'Don't think so.'

'We'll miss you, Cookie.'

'We'll all miss each other. We're all going off to separate things aren't we!'

'We will meet up every weekend though, at the VG, for the rest of our lives, yeah!'

'Am I invited?'

'Absolutely Dicky son, tent-builder extraordinaire!'

'Am I an honononorararary member…'

'What was that?'

'Was that a remix?'

'I'm pissed lads! *Honorary* member of the gang?'

'Defo!'

There was noise behind them then, and the sound of someone opening a can.

'Lads, *lot* of drink you've got here!'

'You just helping yourself are you?'

'That a problem like?'

'Wayne, you okay?'

'Yeah Hedz, you?'

'Good, yeah!'

'This is all a bit bent!'

'How's that?', asked Foz.

'You're sitting in the dark, talking about loving each other, listening to fucking M People?'

Everyone looked at Bucky, who shrugged apologetically.

'Got any grass, Hedz?'

'Erm..a bit for just us lot.'

'Are you telling Wayne 'no'?'

The group looked around, and in the dark noticed other

silhouettes between their tents. Cookie started to get up, but Lee firmly pushed down on his arm.

'So the answer you were looking for *was*…?' asked Wayne.

'Yes, mate. Here you go.'

'Cheers. Bye fags!'

'Wait there's twenty quid's worth there!'

'Do you want us to take all the booze as well? Mark me words, I will!'

'Sorry - enjoy I guess…'

'Limpy fucking *wanker*!', added Knacker under his breath.

'Brave of you!'

'Did you search for the hero inside yourself, Knacky?'

'None of us did anything, so don't have a go at *him*!'

'Check they've gone, will you? Don't want that lot reappearing. Thought it was too good to be true not having any run-ins the whole Summer.'

'I didn't know they existed outside of the subway by the school.'

'Imagine that, leaving school and spending all your days just hanging around it, starting on younger kids and stealing their shit!'

'Why are you taking shit *to* school?'

'Haha, for *you* to talk!'

'Touche!'

'Can't see them, but they've not walked up the road to the exit, you know!'

'Well, where the fuck *did* they go then? We're miles away from town!'

'They're gone, *that's* what matters.'

'Turn that music off mate - we'll head to bed, yeah?'

'Guess so…'

'What a downer!'

'It's been a class day - don't let *that* spoil it!'

'Well, I won't!', said Gaz. 'We're kings of our world, lads!'

'What does that even mean, you say it all the time!'

'Yeah, we're not Kings of the world, there's always someone or something to spoil it!'

'A deranged teacher, a psychotic bully…'

'Hey, we beat that fucking deranged teacher!'

'I mean my *real* world, lads, is *awful*. It's abusive, and toxic, but this is *our* world, it's what we make it. When we were little we would imagine we were knights on horses fighting dragons in the school yard...you all remember that?'

'I do, yeah!'

'Well that was *our* world, wasn't it. And we ruled it. No matter what happened, when the dragons became football, then the yard became the boaty, and the swords became these fucking joints I rolled earlier...'

'You fucking *legend*, Gaz!!!'

'King Gaz! King of *our* world!'

They hoisted Gaz, with an arm in plaster and a face like roadkill, up in the air and marched him around the inner circle formed by the tents. Bucky passed up a 'crown' made of cigarette papers stuck to the plastic four-way handcuffs that came on top of cans of lager. Mitch played an imaginary trumpet. Kev mimed playing a big bass drum.

-

As they packed up the last of their things, and threw their empty bottles and cans into two bin bags that Dicky had had the sense to bring because he actually went camping, Gaz stood holding the railings, looking down at the town below, with his back to them.

'We're setting off, Gaz mate!'

'Yeah...I'll catch up.'

'You okay?'

'I'll catch up.'

Lee shrugged and picked up the last tent, noticing Knacker had walked off with just a carrier bag of empty rubbish. By the time Lee reached the huge stone entranceway to the cemetery, he looked back and saw Gaz was coming. A couple of minutes down the road they were all together again, and a few minutes after that they were laughing in the rain. The intention had been to stay all day Sunday but the weather had been so bad through the night that they had changed the plans. Now, to passing cars with windscreen wipers on full, eleven teenage boys in Summer clothing, with burnt red faces and arms, trudged along in uproarious laughter.

Chapter 27: Saturday, 21:00

Bucky had explained what he thought, and now Knacker sat alone on a mouldy bench watching the VG. Behind him, in the estate, the others were knocking on doors. In one hand he held his phone, with the group chat open and the message 'here' already typed to press send. In the other, he now realised, he held his car keys, with the longest key sticking through between the fingers; the rest of the bunch enveloped in a tight fist. When he had done that, he had no idea. He knew why though. It was fear. Pure and icey, it had settled on him as soon as Dave had said he wasn't joining them. They had always been meant to stay together; he knew the others felt that way as well, but now there was no Foz, no Gaz, no Dave. They were looking for someone who, by all accounts, was an animal. An animal with a knife, as well. You'd be more scared of a crocodile if it also had nunchucks, he thought to himself, and tried to smile. He failed.

'Got a light mate?'

'Fuck me...no pal, I don't smoke!'

'You okay?'

'Yeah, sorry, *you* startled me, that's all!'

'No bother then, lardarse!'

'What?'

The man had wandered away, but turned back. 'You got a problem?'

'I've got a great many, but there's no need for *that*!'

He laughed at Knacker, who stuffed his keys into his pocket for fear he would use them if the man came closer, and then just turned and walked into the shop.

His phone suddenly vibrating almost made him drop it.

'Mitch, alright?'

'Yeah, any joy?'

'None of those young'uns, but some guy has just kind of started on me.'

'Want me to come back?'

'No, he's gone in the shop! Weird, aggressive little fella.'

'Not know him?'

'No. How you all getting on?'

'We're into Beechfield now, all trying different doors. Cookie's staying back saying he's *watching the road* but you know why he won't go to a stranger's door!'

'Shit, yeah. I wouldn't!'

'Don't wanna get Fritzl'd!'

'True that. Let me know if you find it!'

'Will do, and you let us know if you see them. And careful with this bloke, *alright*!'

'What's that banging?'

'Fucking shite music! Be *careful*!'

'Yeah yeah, I'll just kick the gimp in his gammy leg and waddle away! Bye!'

Knacker hung up and noticed something as he lowered his illuminated phone back toward his lap. On the bench, amongst a thousand other scratches and carvings, he could make out a round shape followed by a 'z'. It could have been 'Foz', 'Gaz' or an infinity of other options, but he felt a little less scared.

Chapter 28: Saturday, 21:00

'Any luck lads?'
'No mate, next street?'
'Yeah, only the one left!'
'Well, this *is* the way he was running!'
'And where they ran to after the fight!'
'And it's the *only* place he could have gone fast enough when Kev saw him in the shop!'
'That's right!'
'Gotta be in here somewhere then!'
'You lot had some funny responses?'
'Few pissed off people getting disturbed at whatever-o'clock it is!'
'No, I described the kid and a couple of people have clearly known who he is but said they didn't know.'
'Yeah, I've had the same.'
'Or they're friendly then suddenly want you gone!'
'That's just because they think *you're* begging for change, Kev!'
'Mitch, ring Knacker and tell him we've got one more street will you?'
'Will do!'

The group rounded the top of the street and separated to a house each, with Cookie hanging back in the middle of the road and Mitch at the corner calling Knacker.

At the end house, muffled music emanating from between every brick it seemed, Hughesy knocked once and the door was opened instantly. Cookie turned and looked as he was doing as every door opened. Bucky had not yet entered the garden further down the street when he saw Cookie run toward the house at the top. Lee had knocked on his door, but turned to see why Cookie and Bucky were running. As the door opened, Lee was already out of the gate.

Hughesy was knocking loudly on the door which the kid had just closed.

'We *need* to talk to you!'
'Open this door!', shouted Cookie.
'Piss off! Leave me alone! I had nothing to do with what

happened to Gary!'

'We don't think you did!'

'What do you want then?'

'That's Gaz's watch! He was wearing it the night he was stabbed, not his silver one. The police didn't find his phone or that watch though!'

'I don't get it!'

The window above opened, and bass echoed across the street. A cigarette end was flicked out, and then a hand reached to pull the window shut again.

'Oy!', shouted Kev.

'Sean's face looked down, confused at first and then terrified as he recognised Cookie, and he disappeared. Momentarily, the kid's brother appeared at the window.

'The *fuck* do you lot want?'

'We need to have a word with you!'

Behind them, Mitch started shouting something and walking over briskly, but the noise drowned him out!

'Get to fuck you old cunts, hew!'

'How what?'

'Just fuck off!'

'Open the door!'

'Nee chance, Grandad!'

Hughesy bent down and started talking through the letterbox, as Cookie glared up at the window. Lee continued to talk to the older teenagers upstairs as Mitch came through the gate. Hughesy continued to talk to the kid as Mitch said 'ask him if his Da's got a limp!'

'What did he just say to our boy?', from above.

'Yeah', through the letterbox.

'Is his name *Wayne*?'

Hughesy passed it on. Then looked up at Mitch and nodded.

'Open this *fucking cunting bastard twatting* door *now* you little *shits*!', screamed Cookie, before charging forward as blue lights began to illuminate the street.

Chapter 29: Saturday, 21:10

'You too fat to get up and fuck off?'

'Who's off? She *your* Ma?'

'You what?'

'Just piss off and leave me alone, man!'

'Wait a fucking minute! Fat cunt, thinks he's funny, you're the one who had a go at my youngest!'

'What? The kid by the VG?'

'Yeah, clever cunt! Sent our boy down to give you a kicking and said you were curled up in a ball, which is what you are anyway, crying like a little *bitch*! Said you fucking shit *yourself*!'

'You sent your kids back here to start trouble?'

'I sent them here to fucking act like men, not take shit from you!'

'Father of the year must be on the horizon soon! I seem to recall they *all* got a crack!'

'Do you now? How about we see who the man is here, eh?'

Knacker felt his hand search for the keys again, but something else happened instead. His brain told him not to make that mistake. He lifted his phone.

'Stop tapping on that, *nobody's* going to stick up for you! Aye, they got a kicking, but we had the last laugh didn't we?'

'*We?*'

'Yeah, see once my youngest was in bed I brought the others back out. Me best mate's lad was the big'un you see, the one who got his face bust off a wall! My eldest, he's a proper man, growing up strong, not like the little weak one! I've tried toughening him up but it's no good. Some old cunt even rang and gave him a job, said he was a lovely lad. Fucking joke, doin' things for nowt for people! He's a *mug*!'

'So what did *you* do?', asked Knacker, starting to get to his feet.

'What we *had* to. Someone hurts *you*, you hurt them *more*. Watched you a bit, saw you all sitting there on that grass, then your mate came running over and banged on the shop door. He picked something up, looked at us and I said 'oy', but he just ran off.

'Gaz?'

'Who gives a fuck.'

'I do.'

'I said a fuck, not a ten pound shit! Saw you actually, going to the car, now I think of it. We walked along behind you as you and that little one pulled away! We could see that big cunt walking off with two others, so we went 'round the lake and started catching up to them. Saw another two walking arms around their shoulders, fucking *benders*, crossed the path further back behind us, and we nearly turned back for them. Don't want fucking disease-spreading homos in *my* town, you know!'

'But you didn't?'

'Naw, Sean's Dad, that's the big one, he wanted to get your big mate so we stayed on them. Always under the trees along behind the school, you know. Always out of sight. Then they went into the estate and we thought we'd lost *all* three of them!'

His phone began to ring, and he pressed a button then thrust it back into his pocket. 'Doesn't fucking work, piece of shit!'

Two figures came around the end of the street, behind the man, and silently moved toward him. Some sense of relief came over Knacker.

'Then you found Gaz?'

'We did, aye. Told the bairn to slice him up but he wouldn't, he's still young! So I *had* to', he clicked a knife open with a slithering sound, 'and he even went to put up a fight at first, you know! Daft cunt.'

'You don't need that!'

'Oh, I know. I just like it! It felt good, watching your friend's eyes in the dark - he tried to grab my arm and at first he didn't let go, but then I felt the wave of life fuck off out of him!'

'You *don't* care? Why would you do *that* to someone? For what? Gaz wasn't even there when the fight happened!'

'Hurts all of *you*, doesn't it!'

'Yeah, it does! Worse that his life was taken, that of a

good man, by a spineless little fucking *coward* though!'

At that, he rushed forward at Knacker, who stepped back and brought a massive fist down flush on his temple.

'Fuck me, Knacker! Will you stop being a bloody hero!', gasped Mitch.

The policeman bent down and moved away the knife.

Chapter 30: Saturday, 21:20

'Wayne's under arrest on suspicion of murder. We've got his sons in cuffs as well, and their friends, even a young girl!'

'The youngest lad had nothing to do with it!'

'Well, the oldest definitely did - he's already admitted he went knowingly to cause harm, but that he didn't know the father had a weapon. He was then sent back by the father to get Gary's valuables, which as you know, were just a watch and a faulty mobile phone.'

'So *he* did it? The Da!'

'Yeah, but I think there's been a lot of fear instilled in those boys - they would do whatever he said.'

'Like a lot of people?'

'A lot of people around here, yes! Family have a history of violence and intimidation.'

'Apart from the boys though, he's likely to claim innocence and it's his word against yours.'

'It's *not* actually.'

Knacker opened an app on his phone, which had two images in it. One was his large face, close up in a well lit kitchen, the other was too dark to make out.

'Watch *this*!'

Knacker pressed the image and a greenish picture began to move. He turned up the volume.

'...doin' things for nowt for people! He's a *mug*!'

The tinny sound of Wayne's voice brought a smile to the officer's face. 'Is this...is this what just happened? *In* night vision? *With* sound?'

'It is yeah, it's an impressive piece of kit!'

'What is it?'

'Baby monitor...', Knacker reached below the bench and pulled it out.

'You really are a hero, mate', beamed Mitch.

Chapter 31: 1974

Both seven year old boys screamed.

As he was dragged home, people kept nodding their greetings to his father, ignoring his young, scared eyes.

Shoved through the front door, the image of his friend's face, streamed with tears and snot, being held back by his mother until they were out of their garden, was imprinted on his mind. He was disgusted, but he didn't know that was what the feeling he experienced was called. The sounds of boot on skull on stone kept echoing through his ears, scoring their memory into his mind.

'Listen here, Wayne, you mark me words people will fucking respect *you* now! Nobody fucks with *us*! Someone hurts ours and we hurt theirs more, got *that*?'

Wayne sat silently.

'Wipe those tears away you're not a fucking *girl*! Get cleaned up!'

'I think I need to see a doctor...m-my leg...'

'Fuck that! Don't be a little pussy.' There was a banging on the door. 'Mouth shut. Get upstairs!'

In his bedroom, next to the remains of his door, Wayne held the photograph, shattered now, and listened to the muffled voices from downstairs. At one point he heard his Dad raise his voice and say 'prove it, then', but the rest was inaudible, indecipherable and drowned behind bootskullstone.

As he sobbed silently, the scorching agony enveloping his shin, the sounds and looks of fear were replaced by one thought: spinning, repeating, constant.

Over the days, then weeks that followed, this thought grew and grew. His friend wouldn't speak to him, and they moved shortly after while there was still no news on whether his Dad was going to wake up. He started getting let in the queue in the shop, he started being offered sweets by the kids at school, and the thought grew and took hold in his mind with cancerous, clinging claws. A kid he'd been scared of - a huge lad, a year or two above him - started hanging around, and they started to seek out trouble. The police never returned, although they had been knocking on doors and talking to a lot of people in the area. The thought blossomed. After a month or so, he stopped using the big stick he'd found to help him walk, but it stayed at his dad's front door long after he'd left home, right up until the day he died.

The thought that lingered, that malingered, that became malignant, was of all those people, having seen what his Dad had just done, nodding hello. Not running to stop him. Not even with eyes of disgust. Their eyes had said hello, but also sparkled with fear, and that had proven more powerful than *anything*.

Their nothing had become his everything.

Chapter 32: Canter

'Dads, dads, dads!'
'Not yet!'
'Nearly matey!'
'Where am I sitting? Over there?'
'Yeah, Hughesy. How's it going?'
'Canny, yeah, looking forward to how much of a meltdown you'll be having.'
'When's due date?'
Next Friday, and I'm sh...bricking it! I've made it through all the bad stuff these two told me to prepare for, but now there's gonna be a life to take care of, not just a psychotic mutant to avoid!'
'That wasn't the bad stuff. That starts approximately next Friday!'
'Don't be a c-word!'
'Crayfish?'
'Condom?'
'Catastrophe?'
'You're already one of them, Knacker! Where's the right side of you gone?'
'Seven stone dropped now lads, you'll have to stop calling me Knacker!'
'Fuck that, you still look like one but now just a forty-year-old saggy long one!'
'That's happened to all of you as well?'
'Yeah, looks like they've had an argument and my left one is moving out to my knee!'
'I thought it was a diet thing - I hadn't seen this happen gradually, had I!'
'Drinks, lads.'
'Cheers, Dave!'
'Is it just us?'
'Yeah, the others didn't want to talk about kids all night. Hedz said he might pop down but he's been preparing disadvantaged kids for a performance of Grease at the Community Centre.'
'He's still a bad person, right?'

'Guess so, yeah! But how many good people are narcissistic arseholes? Maybe he's just doing his best in the best way he can - like all of us.'

'Speaking of...best way to not be shit at babying?'

'Right. All that stuff we told you about pregnancy, it stays for quite a while.'

'No, come on?'

'It does, dude!'

'But also you've got this thing that people will say is cute, when they all look like shaved monkeys that have been forced through a keyhole face first, for at least a month or two!'

'And that thing will make a noise like you've never heard. It's not loud, it's just fucking piercing! You will hear it and start to react, but Sarah will already be on her way.'

'Yeah the Ma gains this telepathic sense, like she smells a cry starting!'

'And the fact that you were never ever first to hear it will be entirely your fault because you are an awful human who deliberately left that baby crying for three point one seconds!'

'That's not it though. After a second or two you will always go for the kid. The woman will have this ability to ignore it completely if she's doing something. Just tune the little twat out, just like that! And you'll be like, in the middle of something, and she'll be sat right next to the ugly little air raid siren on her phone blanking the fuck out of it.'

'You'll ask why and she'll say 'got to learn we won't pick it up every time it cries' but that only applies when it's not you who should be picking it up!'

'I'm glad we're not getting a baby!'

'I'm glad I've acquired oven ready little walking, talking bastards!'

'Still no fun, Mitch?'

'They are trained, professional, sly little cockblockers!'

Dave tried to light the candles on the table with a match, which wouldn't work.

'Here', said Cookie, handing over two lighters.

'Why've you got these?'

'Had them months, keep putting them in my pocket every time I'm seeing you lot!'

'Why is this getting romantic, Dave?'

'Haha it's not, it's just nice. And we'll have no more candles soon!'

'Get on your wick?'

'Very good...for you! No, we've got to childproof the whole house for the checks.'

'Really? When's that?'

'Next Friday as well - don't want to get ahead of ourselves but we're quite a long way through the process now.'

'Wait, is that why I couldn't get the toilet seat up?'

'It's just a safety catch, you should have been able to still.'

'Couldn't.'

'At first, or at all?'

'At all!'

'Then where did you have a wee?'

'Garden!'

'Mate, man!'

'So, once you've got through the monkey stage, then it starts moving and eating and I shit you not it will only ever move toward dangerous things and only ever eat if it can try and choke itself!'

'I remember mine gagging on yoghurt! Fucking liquid!'

'And there's the poo!'

'Oh, I've heard all about the different colours and consistencies, the smells, the fact it can shoot out like a dart...'

'Oh mate, I meant *hers*!'

'Eh?'

'She's gonna do a lot of pushing next week, with possibly drugs relaxing parts of her - don't be surprised if you find yourself scraping dried shit off her back when she can finally stagger to the shower!'

'Food's served, boys!', said Michael as he came into the room. 'What's wrong with Cookie?'

'Nothing, Micko!'

'*Michael*!'

Chapter 33: Coffees

'Pass the sugar mate.'
'Here. So, it's been an eventful few months for us lads!'
'Yeah, should we just address the elephant in the…'
'Knacker! My name's Knacker!'
'It's not!'
'I prefer it, awful as it is it's still what my best mates call me!'
'No, I mean, it's Mountain!'
'Haha yeah we're changing it for ya!'
'By weed poll!'
'Thanks, lads!'
'It'll sound better when the missus shouts it out now too!'
'Or 'Mountain's Bike' if she fancies a nickname!'
'Better fucking not, lads - she'd *kill* me!'
'Haha anyway...the elephant...I do want to talk about Foz, lads!'
'Yeah, it feels like because of Gaz we kind of got distracted.'
'Distraction from grief is a good thing, no?'
'Not if it's for *more* grief!'
'And not if it means you don't process it properly.'
'We said our goodbyes and all that, but I've been *struggling*, like I said.'
'Have you been doing that hypnosis shit still?'
'Yeah!'
'Chicken!'
'Bok-bok...just kidding! It's helping me deal with the stresses of the day, relaxing, even sleeping but it's not helping get my head around it all properly, and piss off with the Catchphrase jokes!'
'I've said this before, but I don't think it *needs* to get gotten around, or boxed off, or dealt with!'
'What do you mean?'
'I think profound loss is with you all the time, and admitting it, talking about it, sharing it, is all natural. If it's hanging over us it's meant to - it may not be nice to deal with, and struggling is real and normal - but it lingers and creeps into

every memory because we cared *so much* for him. For them both.'

'I know we see them as very different types of grief, as if Gaz had no say and Foz did, but I think depression *is* a psychotic bully with a flickknife!'

'Absolutely!'

'It watches and stalks and takes and takes - until there's nothing left to appease it, you can't pay it off any more, and it strikes.'

'Good analogy that, mate!'

'Anal orgy? Dave, Mick?'

'Michael!'

Bucky laughed at his own joke more than the others, who were trying hard to be more mature around the kids. 'I'm just funning! I agree with you mate! Just wish we didn't have to - just wish they were *here*.'

'But *if* they were, and I in no way think there is anything close to a silver lining to this, we wouldn't be together again? Would we, *honestly*?'

'We'd still be clicking thumbs ups and love hearts instead of using actual words! It was so much better when there was no social media…'

'Or when social media meant you had sent a letter to someone!'

'Wait, did you lot not have Facebook when you were kids, hew?'

'How what?'

'No Jake, son. *We* didn't even have mobile phones!'

'Wow. How did you meet up and stuff?'

'Exactly!', said Mountain. 'It was so easy to miss everyone!'

'Ignore him! We just told each other where to be and then went there, and *all* turned up. We said anything we needed to face-to-face with body language and emotion so nothing got misconstrued, and we never had any clue what each other had had for tea!'

'I never knew this. Do they cover this all in History?'

'One day they will. The masquerade revolution they'll call it, when everyone forgot to talk and hug and take the piss and all just hid behind an airbrushed avatar life!'

'You're right it's *not* a silver lining, but it's at least a bit beige that Foz completing suicide brought us together. We've opened up a lot - what did you say about gates or something Lee?'

'I said we were *doors* - needed to open up!'

'That's it! We have, haven't we? Or at least *started* to - perhaps we'll never know but this, now, might be preventing something for someone else. We might have stopped the spiral by being together.'

'Good way to look at it I guess. Any tea left?'

'Yeah, here. Sugar?'

Honeybunny?'

'Piss off.'

'Lads, that Summer I knocked about with you lot when we were kids, that was the best you know! Chris was alive and doing my tits in, the pressures of college and that hadn't started. I wish I'd stayed close to you all over the years!'

'Plenty years for being gay now, Hedz.'

'How come you always make gay jokes, when you know...*they're* gay!'

'I am not gay!', exclaimed Michael in a shrill voice.

'Jake, we were raised in a different time, when making a joke about something didn't mean you were a figure of hatred. We made jokes about everything, the more it made your mates say 'oooh' the better, and *nothing* was off limits.'

'It was a better time, young'un!'

'You could tell by the massive grin on a face if it was a joke or not!'

'Nowadays the snowflakes are the start of an avalanche.'

'There is a very big difference between being called a 'bender' by your mates and having it screamed in your face by a *stranger*, or being kicked to the ground in an alleyway while they shout 'homo'.'

'Right. So you *don't* mind it? From these, I mean?'

'Look', said Michael, 'we live now in a world where most people get their advice from Primark tops, instead of just knowing to 'be kind' in the first place. Because of that, any comment about anything that can be *possibly* perceived as potentially offensive is taboo. Our friend Foz once told me that if we don't insult people we're treating them differently, and as insane as that sounds, it's scarily accurate.'

'So we insult each other as much as possible, in *as many ways as possible*, because we are so *fucking* kind!'

'Language Mitch, man!'

'He's heard all this before. You're nearly fifteen aren't ya, lad?'

'Not him!'

'*They* don't bloody understand!'

'I don't like this 'completing' business.'

'You mean completing suicide?'

'Yeah. I complete waxing the truck - suicide isn't a *job*!', said Dicky.

'Suicide? Completed it, bro!'

'Fuck me when you put it like *that...*'

'Now we're *all* swearing again!'

'I understand changing 'committed' though - it's not a *crime*!'

'What's the alternatives? I agree I don't like 'completed' either. When he said it I felt myself recoil.'

'Suffered?'

'Succumbed to?'

'Maybe.'

'It's just something *else* that the discussion, not ours but the wider one, is focused on instead of dealing with the committed or completed or suffered instances!'

'I don't want to sound preachy...'

'We *need* someone to! We need those people who can stand up and make a difference, not in a religious way but in a humanitarian way!'

'Right, well I will sound preachy then', said Lee. 'We talked about this that night we got the kebabs, when we were down the town yeah, and I think about it a lot. It's *constant*, from schools and the government and on our demon social media and everywhere, that we *have to* look after our mental health!'

'And each others'!'

'Yeah, but most people don't see the *difference* between

mental health and mental illness - everyone wants to talk about spa days and mindfulness as though that helps; yeah that's good for your *mental health* but until people openly talk about, without getting uncomfortable, suicidal thoughts, blackouts, manic episodes...*mental illness*...then we get nowhere. They're *not* the same, and everytime someone is depressed or suicidal and sees or hears someone saying 'we all have mental health' they think they are *not* going through something *specific* to them. They think it's *normal*, that they don't *have to* get help, so they don't *ask* for it because 'everyone is the same'.

'I've started pushing the governors to implement a structured mental health programme, properly timetabled rather than squeezed into the curriculum - I think that's where we have to start as a society!'

'But why are *you* doing it? No offence Hedz, but you're a fucking drug dealer at the end of the day; where's the government on this? Why are we shoulder deep in thousands of lost lives and still not being pulled out?'

'None taken, by the way - I don't know.'

'More coffee anyone?'

'You'll need a new flask, that one's empty!'

'Cheers, Hughesy.'

'No probs. I've been sat here silently lads because I think there's something we're overlooking. You know I visit Foz's Ma, right, and she has told me a couple of times that his dad battled depression his *whole* life.'

'Really?'

'Foz told us this after he had passed away, actually', added Dave.

'Yeah, apparently when he was a kid him and his Mam watched his Dad get beaten to death! They had to move and he didn't die immediately, it was drawn out and *everything* uprooted - but Morris, Foz's Da, he always struggled with it. What about genetics then - can education help if it's passed on and down?'

'Was it passed down, or did Foz learn certain behaviours and ways of dealing with things?'

'Or did Foz just have his own issues, completely separate,

that formed of their own making?'

'Whatever it is, education has to be key.'

'Education starting very young, but for everyone though. Those fifty year olds demonising mental illness need to learn to understand, the nattering grannies not knowing enough about bipolar not to judge the kid on the street need to know more.'

'It is education then but at *every* level - this isn't a school thing it's a home, school, college, uni, workplace thing! And it's two main things, in my opinion, dunno if you will all agree...it's educating people to know where to get help and how to *articulate their need for it* without fear of stigma, and educating other people to know the signs and what to do to help. *Right*?

'We came here for a reason, and we've ended up trying to set the world to rights *again*!'

'Happens every time we come *here*!'

'This will lighten the mood, lads. Foz's Grandma was called Doris.'

'Why's that funny?'

'Wait, and his Da was Morris?'

'Nee way - what was his Grandad called, *Boris*?'

'No, Len!'

'Oh.'

'But just think how close Foz probably came to being named Horace!'

They all laughed then. It felt good. Since they had got to the truth about Gaz, they had been meeting up in smaller groups for food, for drinks and for a lot of heart to hearts, all with plenty laughter. It was the laughter that seemed to be the glue between them, and every sad memory was accompanied by twenty happy ones.

'Before we get down to it, lads, can I just say that I would not have got through all of this fear, and that's what it has been, without *you*.'

'Fear, yeah?'

'Fear of speaking up, fear of looking weak, fear of failing as a parent...' said Cookie.

'Fear of pain, of loss, of forgetting...'

'...of remembering and feeling too low...'

'Fear of *letterboxes*!'

'Fear of losing more of you!'

'There is so much fear for us all, that if you don't have the people you rely on then it can *easily* take over!', finished Cookie.

'I'm scared if we don't get a move on we'll have that fucking sunburn again!'

'Haha right okay, sorry - I'm done being a big gay bear! Love you, lads!'

'Thought you were done?'

'Kev, pressa de play!'

Kev turned on his chair and pulled the ghettoblaster forward. He pressed play and '*We've come so far and we've reached so high*' resounded off the white stone pillars behind them.

'What is *that*?' asked Jake.

'Something Kev's Da kept in the attic of natural history!'

'Right lads, on *your* feet!'

'Who's gonna say a few?'

'Not me this time', said Lee, 'I'll hold the ashes though!'

'Jake, you got yours?'

'Yeah, I've got him!'

'Okay', said Mitch, 'I'd like to say goodbye to Gaz. We're all here to say a proper goodbye, because we never got the chance. He was taken far too early, but he made a difference to *all* of us; our lives wouldn't have been as much fun without Gaz to grow up with. It's just a shame we don't grow old *with* him. He made a real difference to our boy Jake here as well. He was funny, loyal and let's not pretend he was the sharpest tool in the box, but he was essential. Like a hammer!'

'Mitch hasn't got Lee's way with analogies!'

'He wouldn't have understood the comparison anyway! He's gone, but we love him in a totally straight way and always will, our *King*, and now wherever they are, him and Foz can knock about together, one of them knocking and the other *not* running, getting stoned and drunk for eternity - lads forever!'

'Well, *that* was beautiful!'

'A eulogy mentioning how thick he was?'

'Let's be realistic lads, he once told me he'd ordered something from 'amazing' and it took me ages to click on he couldn't read *Amazon* properly - it was one of his best qualities!'

'Come here all of you!'

The twelve of them stood together, arms around each other's shoulders except Michael who held his and Dave's toddler on his chest, facing forward. They formed a rough semi-circle facing the railings overlooking the town below, as *'There's a road going down the other side of this hill'* lifted on the breeze.

Lee and Jake lifted the lids on the metal tins they both held, the sun flashing against Jake's silver watch, as everyone else sang in their worst falsetto voices *'ne-eeeeeeever'*.

They threw the ashes forward into the air simultaneously, through the railings, only for the breeze to sweep them back and to the right, dusting Mitch at the far end of the semi-circle.

'Fuck, man!'

'I've got Gaz in me mouth! I've got Gaz *in me mouth*! Pass the flask!'

'Empty mate. Shame!'

'Fuck off! Someone got a drink...*here*!'

'Don't you fu...bloody dare!', shouted Cookie, as Mitch unscrewed the lid and swigged.

'Urgh, what is *that*?'

'Breast milk!'

'I've got Gaz *and* Sarah in me gob! Me face is full of life *and* death!'

Once the laughter died down, and Dicky had reluctantly let Mitch drink his water, which he declined taking back, they stood in silence for a moment.

'Right, throw all the flasks and chairs in there and we'll make a move.'

'Bairn still asleep, mate?'

'Oh yeah, these carriers make them feel proper snuggled

in to your heartbeat, Gareth will be out for hours!'

'Still can't believe you called him Gareth. Were you not there when Gaz confirmed his name?'

'Cookie was inside the house of a thousand corpses at the time! It was in the street just after Bucky and me had spoken to death!'

'It's still a nice little tribute, but that kid must be the only Gareth born in the last thirty years! Can you not use his middle name?'

'No, *definitely* not!'

'Why?'

'It's another tribute!'

'Who to?' asked Mountain.

'Yeah come on, what's his *full* name?'

'Gareth *Knacker* Cook!'

Chapter 34: Cem

'We're setting off, Jake lad!'
'Yeah...I'll catch up.'
'You *okay*?'
'I'll catch up, Lee.'

Holding onto the flaking, rusted railings, Jake looked across the town. He'd never really appreciated peace or calm until the last few months, and wanted to hold onto this moment a while longer. The sun beat down and he could hear the creaking of the wheelbarrow as Mitch wheeled it away.

'I'm still not overjoyed we spread Cliff up here, you know', said Bucky as he and Lee walked away from Jake.

'It's what that kid *needed* though - and he *only* knew a version of Gaz's da that we didn't. Gaz obviously got to know that version as well. You know after that Summer when we camped up here, when he had the black eye and his arm in that cast, I *never* saw Gaz with a mark on him again. We both went on the same apprenticeship, and he relaxed loads. Stayed on the dope though.'

'Fair enough - seems like a good lad. Nice of his carers to let him come up here today.'

'Yeah, but they've been parked there watching the *whole* time!'

'Where? Oh, I didn't even notice that. Good on them.'

'Yeah? What you mean?'

'Well, you've come in short shorts, mate. Linen ones. Wouldn't let my kid near you!'

'For fuck's sake, man - you know what...'

As they caught up to Mitch pushing the wheelbarrow, who seemed to be struggling to keep the chairs, rubbish and drinks containers all in place, a rogue silver metal flask, much like you used to be able to buy in Boyes, fell from the side. Landing in probably the only piece of dog poo in the whole cemetery, the resulting splash dashed up the outside of Lee's bare left leg. Bucky and Mitch stared at him and both walked away, the laughter getting louder the further they went.

'Well, I don't think he'll wear short shorts again!'
'Yeah, suppose.'
'He's always getting himself in the shit!'
'Similar note, hope Dave washed this thing out before we put our stuff in it.'
'Why?'
'It's what I pissed in in his garden!'
'If I've got Gaz, Sarah and *you* in my mouth...mark me words!'
'Semisonic, by the way, who sang Closing Time!'
'Was it?'
'Yeah.'
'Thought that was an Oasis song?'

They reached the stone gates of the cemetery, just about catching up to the others, as Lee rejoined them.

He looked back, and at first it looked like a young Gaz was behind him, walking up the long path. Bucky and Mitch started singing *'every new beginning comes from some other beginning's end'*.

Gaz: 1995

Holding onto the new railings, Gaz stared at the town below. He traced his way from the VG, to the school, to the park and all the way to his house. The rain battered down on his sunburn like tiny blades, but he thought it still looked darker over his than anywhere else.

'We're setting off, Gaz mate!'

'Yeah...I'll catch up.'

'You okay?'

'I'll catch up.'

He listened as Lee picked something up and started to plod away in the mud.

'Cookie wants to kill you. I think they *all* would. So do I. At least this version of you. When I get back I'm ringing the police', he said through the metal bars, 'and you're not going to hurt me *anymore*. I don't *deserve* it. I'm a *King*. No matter what has happened, I've always had my friends and they're all going to move on. I don't want them to go. I know they have to but last night I slept because I know *nothing* can truly hurt me when I've got *them*!'

With that, Gaz spat through the gap, with an anger and venom that the boys had never seen, and clenched his fists around the poles.

'We should stay together - lads forever!'

He turned and began to walk quickly, gaining on Lee before he'd even left the cemetery.

another end

What people said about Nine Doors (that I did not bribe)

- The one liners and friendly ridiculing between the characters makes you giggle and imagine your own group of friends and the entire story made me feel nostalgic and filled with happy memories from those years. The overall message of the book made me think about my own group of friends and reminded me that what we see on social media isn't always the whole truth and so it's important to send that text / message and try to catch up when we can.
- A nostalgic journey that took me right back to my teenage years in the mid 90's, when we played Knocker Door Run, caused havoc and had friends for life. Incredibly well written in the only way it could of been wrote to do the book justice.
- A funny gripping story with a important message that hopefully all that read it will take on board and act on.
- Well this book took me back to being an absolute idiot in the 90's. I read the book in one day as I couldn't put it down. It will have you belly laughing and also crying which is a wonderful mix. It leaves you wanting to know more about the group of lads in the story. Fully recommend this book.
- Read this in a couple of days. Such a nostalgic trip through my youth, growing up and trying to keep that childish humour alive. It hits hard at times and catches you by surprise, and the overall message is an important one. Loved it.
- Took me back to some embarrassing yet brilliant times, yet also showed the importance of good friends. Really hope that there will be a second book to see how the blokes get on in the future.
- The beginning grips you & draws you in, ending did bring a tear to my eye & leaves you wanting to know what happens next, i laid thinking about it for quite a while after. You just don't know whats around the corner so If you need to talk pick up the phone & ask for help, if you think someone is struggling, check in on them....stay safe.
- Once I picked it up I couldn't put it down until I was finished.
Dealing with the subject of mental health can be something that's difficult to put lightly, yet the author manages to keep us laughing whilst conveying such an important message using only a few memorable sentences.
In the age of social media I'm glad this book give me a little reminder that not everything you see is the real world.
- The author makes no bones that there is a heavily autobiographical element to this book, but the appeal here is universal. Anyone who was lucky enough to have a close-knit group of pals in their teenage years will appreciate this book's message, which is both bitter (that time moves on and things change) and sweet (that times move on and so much stays the same). Loved it.

What happened to Foz may not yet be explicit - it doesn't need to be. Your friends and family love you.

If you're feeling like you want to die, it's important to tell someone. Help and support is available right now You do not have to struggle with difficult feelings alone. www.ManHealth.org.uk are available, or:

Phone a helpline

These free helplines are there to help when you're feeling down or desperate.

Samaritans - for everyone

Call 116 123

Campaign Against Living Miserably (CALM)

Call 0800 58 58 58 – 5pm to midnight every day

Papyrus – for people under 35

Call 0800 068 41 41 – 9am to midnight every day

Childline – for children and young people under 19

Call 0800 1111 – the number will not show up on your phone bill

SOS Suicide of Silence – for everyone

Call 0300 1020 505 – 9am to midnight every day

Message a text line

If you do not want to talk to someone over the phone, these text lines are open 24 hours a day, every day.

Shout Crisis Text Line – for everyone

Text "SHOUT" to 85258

YoungMinds Crisis Messenger – for people under 19

Text "YM" to 85258

Talk to someone you trust

Let family or friends know what's going on for you. They may be able to offer support and help keep you safe.

There's no right or wrong way to talk about suicidal feelings – starting the conversation is what's important.

Who else you can talk to

If you find it difficult to talk to someone you know, you could:

- call a GP – ask for an emergency appointment
- call 111 out of hours – they will help you find the support and help you need
- contact your mental health crisis team – dependent on your local area